Thomas Chapman

Contentment

And other Poems

Thomas Chapman

Contentment
And other Poems

ISBN/EAN: 9783744765626

Printed in Europe, USA, Canada, Australia, Japan

Cover: Foto ©Andreas Hilbeck / pixelio.de

More available books at **www.hansebooks.com**

Contentment

AND

Other Poems.

BY

THOMAS CHAPMAN

[JOSEPH.]

———

KELSO:
J. & J. H. RUTHERFURD, 20, SQUARE.
1883.

Contents.

	Page.
CONTENTMENT	1
THE GREEN WOODS OF BORTHWICK	3
AULD JACOB TAIT...	5
BURNS	6
ADIEU TO SCOTLAND	8
TO BEAUTY	10
THE GOD OF BABYLON	12
THE BEGGAR'S BALL	14
THE GIPSY SPREE...	15
AUTUMN	17
TO A LADY	18
MY WEE LASSIE MARY	19
A FAREWELL	20
THE HAWTHORN TREE	21
MAY	22
DENHOLM...	ib.
THE WOODS	23
MY AULD CLAY BIGGIN'	24
THE MAIDEN SPRING	25
DELIA	26
THE LARK	27
THE SOUL	28
GOD IS HERE	29
SEPTEMBER	30
DEPARTED MAID	32
TAKE FROM MINE EYES	33
THE SNOWDROP	34
WINTER	35
YOUNG YEAR'S DAY	37
TEARS	38
THE GREEN HILLSIDE	40

iv CONTENTS.

	Page.
THE PRIDE O' TEVIOT	41
MY DARLING MAID	42
NO MORE OF YOUR BELLES	44
THE HEID	45
A LUMP IN THE THROAT	47
'TWILL SUNE BE WINTER NOO	49
THE CREATOR	50
WHAT IS MAN?	51
THE HEART	52
THE AUTUMN LEAF	53
NAE FLOWERS IN WINTER	54
SPRING	55
THE GOWANS	56
THE SNOWDROPS	57
A HARVEST PRAYER	58
THE FLOWERS O' SPRING	60
THE HEDGEROWS	61
A WEE SWEET FLOWER	62
THE QUEEN OF MAY	63
THE SWALLOWS	64
JOCKIE	65
SUMMER	66
WEE WILLIE	67
DAUGHTER OF BABYLON	68
THE BEGGARS	70
WHEN I WAS YOUNG	71
THE NOTES O' THE CUCKOO	72
ELLA	73
BONNIE MARY	74
WEEL DAE I MIND	75
GATHERING FLOWERS	77
WOMAN	ib.
AUTHOR OF ALL	79
MARRIED LIFE	80
WATERING THE DAISIES	82
DEAD ARE THE FLOWERETS	83
THAT DAY I LEFT THE BOWMONTSIDE	84
LINES ON CHARLES HAIG, ATTONBURN	85
THE CREATURES OF A DAY	87
SIMMER'S AWA'	88

	Page.
THE REMNANT	89
THE GREEN VALE O' BOWMONT	90
TIME	91
QUEEN ESTHER	92
THE MUMMY KINGS	94
MY PLAID	96
THE LAMMIES	98
THE WOODS O' TEVIOT	99
THE CAPON TREE	100
UNCO MERRY	101
LAND OF MIST	103
HERDIN' DAYS	104
MY FAVOURITE FLOWERS	105
THE BLOW O' THE HAWTHORN	106
THE MAY-TIME	107
ALL BARDS ARE POOR	108
CARLYLE AT THE GRAVE OF HIS WIFE	110
YOUTH AND TIME	111
THE ZEPHYR	112
PUIR RAGGED DAVIE	113
MERRY JOCK	115
HELEN'S LAMENT	116
JESSIE	117
THE FROG	ib.
THE THRUSH	118
SPRING	120
SUMMER	121
AURORA BOREALIS	122
DENHOLM DEAN	ib.
NEW YEAR'S DAY	123
ST. KILDA	125
TEVIOTDALE	126
THE VOICE OF GOD	128
LIFE	129
WHAT IS LIFE?	131
THE HAWTHORN O' THE GLEN	132
THE MOUNTAIN STREAM	133
SECOND LOVE	134
LIZZIE	ib.
BOWMONTSIDE	135

	Page.
My Native Land	136
The Angel of Death	138
Hermitage	139
The Winter Time	140
The Maid o' Woodfit	141
May with the Hazel Eyes	142
Among the Birks	143
Life	145
The White King	146
Ireland	147
Slitrig Bella	148
She Prays for Me	150
An Honest Dog	ib.
Joanna	152
Met Her by Chance	ib.
The Last Day o' the Year	153
The Poisoned Cup	155
Kisses	156
The Crucifixion	157
The Sabbath Day	158
The Yarrow Herd	159
My Faither's Fireside	160
The Canty Folk o' Bowmontside	162
I Weary for the Simmer	163
The Auld Laird	164
New Year's Day	165
Wee Tommy	167
The New Year	ib.
Jean's Lament	169
Still I Miss One	170
Auld Coins	171
Willie's Far frae Bowmont	172
My Auld Friends	174
The Brier Bush	175
The White Steeds	ib.
Sergeant Readdie, late of Jedburgh	177
Adieu, my Friend	179
A Mother's Flower	181
Auld Geordie	ib.
Tom Brown	183

	Page.
HEATHER JOCK	183
SCOTLAND	184
WHO IS HE?	186
THE BUTTERFLIES	188
SPRING	189
THE BEAUTIFUL SPRING	190
I MISS HER	192
THE WATERS OF LOVE	193
THE LINTIE	194
THE YEARS OF MEN	195
MARY M'LEOD, WILTON	196
LIEUTENANT SCOTT DOUGLAS	197
THE WEATHER	198
THE BLIGHTED ROSE	199
THE MIDGE AND THE FLEE	201
KINGS ON HIGH	202
JOHN CAMPBELL, BAKER, HAWICK	203
THE SNAIL	204
THE FLOWER O' KALE	205
THOMAS THOMSON, LATE SHEPHERD, MELLENDEAN, SPROUSTON	206
MY LITTLE LAMBIE	208
THE BARMAID	209
PATIE	210
THE DEID LICHT	211
THE AULD FISH POCK	213
FICKLE FORTUNE	214
IN MEMORIAM—WILLIAM MARTIN	216
EMMA	219
GET GOLD, PURE GOLD	220
DAVID TAIT, KIRK YETHOLM	221
KEEPER JOCK	223
A WANTER CROUSE	224
MAN	225
THE ROSES	227
POOR MAN	228
THE ROYAL STAPLERS	230
THE BERWICKSHIRE SHEPHERD, WALTER CHISHOLM	231
BACHELOR WILLIE	233
PRINCE NAPOLEON	234

	Page.
THE SWALLOWS	235
THE BOWMONT HILLS	236
MY ALBUM	237
MY MOTHER	238
DECEMBER	240
THE PASSING YEAR	241
THE LATE SERGEANT ROBERT AINSLIE	242
THE APPROACH OF WINTER	243
THE WIND KING	245
THE TENTIE HERD	246

CONTENTMENT.

CONTENTMENT, come, why fliest thou from me ?
My bosom friend and mistress ever be ;
Why do I pine, why murmur or regret ?
When thou art absent, thus I ever fret.

Without thee I am rack'd with cares, and torn,
For all who live have got, like Paul, a thorn ;
Had I but wings, from cares away I'd flee :
O smile, my fair one—smile, and come to me.

Come to my bosom ; lo, the daisied plain,
Bedrench'd with dew, now wet with genial rain,
Delights my soul, and feasts my wearied eyes,
Still from my heart contentment ever flies.

Of bliss I dream, for it I've great desire,
From this to that, Napoleon-like, aspire ;
Unto the clouds I let my spirit rove,
Next with the brutes I flounder in the grove.

In search of thee from realm to realm I go,
Climb every height, and findeth nought but woe ;
With me, contentment, stay—why from me fly ?
Hear my request, and deign thou to comply.

When I at eve lie down, my frame to rest,
Come thou and nestle, bird-like, in my breast ;
Without thy ointment there is no repose,
And, wanting thee, mine eyelids will not close.

What do I want ?   I've all this life can need ;
But man's a riddle that is ill to read ;
When nauseous cares the bosom wrings,
O'er me, contentment, spread thy silken wings.

Oh, make me happy ?   If on earth there be
True happiness, bestow thou it on me ;
Point out the path wherein it may be found ;
To perfect bliss no king was ever crowned.

All have got something which doth them annoy,
But why should man his peace of mind destroy ;
One bitter drop the cup of life may sour,
And oft our hopes are blasted as a flower.

For there is much us mortals to torment,
And patient Job through grief his mantle rent ;
In heaven at first there discontent arose
With him they cast out—so the story goes.

Here the contagion Satan spread below—
The fount and father of all human woe—
To happy Eve and guileless Adam went,
And them, in Eden, smote with discontent.

But why should man so grumble or complain,
When he the teats of peace and love might drain ;
From out my heart let discontent be driven,
And to the father of it back be given.

Then come, adored one, to my aching breast,
While I have thee I need no other guest ;
With me, contentment, ever bide and stay,
Rest in my bosom, never fly away.

THE GREEN WOODS OF BORTHWICK.

THE green woods of Borthwick are now in the sere,
And silent the blackbirds that whistled sae clear
Amid the fair blossoms upon the haw tree,
At twilight, when Betsy came tripping to me.
Now simmer is over, and Flora has fled,
And a' the wee flowerets, sae bonnie, are dead ;
For Boreas, rude Boreas, has rifled the bowers
Where I spent wi' my lassie the sweet gloamin' hours.

The green woods of Borthwick, true home of the dove,
Whose cooings sae gentle first woke me to love ;
And tho' the bleak autumn has blighted the scene,
The smiles o' my Betsy are sweet and serene.
Now withered the brackens that we used to pu',
When the bluebells and roses were sprinkled with
    dew;
For Boreas, rude Boreas, has rifled the bowers
Where I spent wi' my lassie the sweet gloamin' hours.

The green woods of Borthwick, tho' robbed of their
    pride,
Within them my Betsy, in blossom, doth bide ;
And when the braw tassels come back to the broom,
We'll rove through the green woods of Borthwick in
    bloom.
Mute and sad is the mavis, for simmer's awa,
And a lilt frae the shilfa I ne'er get ava ;
For Boreas, rude Boreas, has rifled the bowers
Where I spent wi' my lassie the sweet gloamin' hours.

The green woods of Borthwick with music shall ring,
When the song birds awaken their harps in the spring;
And light-footed fairies shall dance round the tree
At twilight, when Betsy comes tripping to me.
The oak and the alder, laburnum and thorn,
Are reft o' their leaflets, nae wonder I mourn ;
For Boreas, rude Boreas, has rifled the bowers
Where I spent wi' my lassie the sweet gloamin' hours.

Sweet hour o' the gloamin', the dearest and best,
It draws me to Betsy, as bird to its nest ;
And close to my bosom, enraptured, I'll strain
My Betsy at twilight, tho' simmer be gane.
The beauties o' simmer frae Borthwick are sped,
And a' the wee flowerets, sae bonnie, are dead ;
For Boreas, rude Boreas, has rifled the bowers
Where I spent wi' my lassie the sweet gloamin' hours.

AULD JACOB TAIT.

No more shall we see him trip over the lawn
With his basket and rod at evening or dawn ;
The trouts they may sport, and of happiness dream,
No more shall he nibble them out of the stream.

Auld Jacob, poor body, he had the real art
Of fixing his hooks in their jaws or their heart ;
He caught them fu' easy by scores where they jouk ;
Where others found none, aye plenty he took.

Wherever he went he could find a supply,
Be the rivers in flood or their channels near dry ;
He could wile them unto him fu' canna an' slee—
At angling and shooting no marrow had he.

The hares, noo sae wanton, I trow had less fun
When he went abroad with his lurcher and gun ;
He upturned their heels, made them wag in the air,
And it was a queer place if he found not a hare.

With rabbits or snipes he seldom would fash,
For he hated to spend his lead upon trash ;
But to blackgame and moorfowl he was a fell foe,
And they soared unco high if he brought them not low.

But for a' that and a' that with mercy him scan,
For there ne'er was a better or kinder auld man ;
With the world he is done, and this, let me say,
A cantier cock was ne'er laid in the clay.

BURNS.

Upon him let us ever look with clear impartial eye,
For who can read his chequered life and find no tears
    to dry ;
Now, back with me, come let us gaze upon that distant
    morn,
When he, our great immortal bard, in lowly cot was
    born.

E'en now I see wild Boreas lift the thatch from off its
    roof,
And gossip, too, that read the lines within his infant
    loof ;
Since then one century and more, away, away has fled,
And Scotland, lavish in his praise, adorns the mighty
    dead.

Ah ! well may Scotland upward rear great monuments
    of art,
For him who nestles like a bird within the Scottish
    heart.
When at the plough the muses put a harp within his
    hand,
He touched its chords, and, lo, a flood of music filled
    the land.

The echoes of that mellow harp in Scotland ever rings,
As if the hand of him who's dead had never left the
    strings ;
Oh, had he stayed behind the plough, and kept from
    out the town,
Some brighter gems than those which shine had sparkled
    in his crown.

In vain regret, but let us gaze at him amongst the
    corn,
Where oft his thoughts, on lark-like wings, above the
    clouds were borne.

Downcast, and wearied of his farm, a gauger see him
    now,
But not so happy and content as when he held the
    plough.

His iron frame and health decays, then view him on
    sick bed,
Still round his brow the berries glow, and with a deeper
    red.
He died beside his bonnie Jean, who watched his
    latest breath ;
And Scotland never knew his worth until she knew his
    death.

ADIEU TO SCOTLAND.

ADIEU to Scotland ; adieu
    Ye woods and rivers grand,
Of you I'll think and often dream
    When in another land.
The ship is waiting for me now
    Upon the foamy tide,
And shortly with it I'll be gone
    Far o'er the ocean wide.

Adieu to Scotland, adieu;
  No wonder that I weep
To leave the land where I was born,
  And where my fathers sleep.
The ship is waiting for me now,
  With sails spread to the wind;
I'll have to go, and must I leave
  Eliza far behind?

Adieu to Scotland, adieu,
  The cradle of brave men,
And maidens fairer than the flower
  In woodland or in glen.
The ship is waiting for me now,
  And soon 'twill bear me on
Across the deep and restless sea
  Unto another zone.

Adieu to Scotland, adieu;
  Eliza, shalt thou stay,
And live contented here at home
  When I am far away?
" Ah, no; ah, no !" the maiden said,
  " No sea shall us divide;
I'll go with thee across the sea,
  Whatever may betide."

Adieu to Scotland, adieu ;
  For it brave Wallace bled,
And doughty Bruce at Bannockburn
  To victory Scotchmen led.
" I fear no grave, I'll dangers brave
  With thee in any land :"
Now on the deck of that stout ship,
  Behold, the lovers stand.

The balmy zephyrs filled the sails,
  And onward sped the ship—
Now up, now down, just as a duck
  Would upward rise and dip.
And as it, swan-like, ploughed the main,
  To those upon the land,
With handkerchiefs they waved adieu
  To Scotland wild and grand.

TO BEAUTY.

Of beauty I have ever been
  A lover great,
And thou, sweet maid, I'll strive to paint,
  Tho' not first-rate ;
Thy breath the fragrance of the year,
  In fullest bloom,

And those long tresses, rich and rare,
    The yellow broom ;
Your voice, a harp by angels strung,
    And those bright eyes
Wring from my bosom many a time
    The heavy sighs.

Thy waist, the slender lily stem,
    Beyond dispute,
In fashion's circle never shone
    A neater foot ;
Your brow the polished marble stone,
    Thy breast the snow,
Your lips red roses, wet with dew,
    In fullest blow.

O maiden, fairest of the land,
    You little know
That thou art thus a goddess great
    To whom men bow ;
And I for one must bend the knee
    At Hymen's shrine,
And tho' you're but an earthly maid,
    You seem divine ;
And all do worship thee as such,
    For many a one
Think you the sweetest flower in bloom
    Beneath the sun.

THE GOD OF BABYLON.

In the flowery plain of Dura see the God of Babylon,
And to worship it the people have been ordered from
    the throne,
When you hear the flute and cornet, and all kinds of
    music rare,
To the sacred plain of Dura hither then you shall repair;

For the king and all his princes have a golden god set
    up,
And to its dedication drink the conscience-damning cup;
When you hear the sound of music, and the heralds
    loudly call,
Remember down before it on your bended knees to fall.

And who bows not to the image shall arouse the mon-
    arch's ire,
So beware, ye Jews and Gentiles, lest your portion be
    the fire ;
There's a burning fiery furnace for those that dare rebel,
'Tis a place of awful torture—oh, its torments none can
    tell.

It is now the time of worship, and some are standing
    there,
And the king beholds they bend not to his god in
    solemn prayer,

And says, "Bow to the image, dare you disobey the
 throne,
And will you not do homage to the god of Babylon?"

"Hear the furnace—make it hotter—dare my subjects
 thus rebel?
Ho, bind and cast them in it;"—but around them was
 a spell,
For they walked within the furnace—not a hair singed
 on their head—
While those who put them in it were scorched and
 lying dead.

Then the astonished king commanded that his people,
 great and small,
Should ever worship after this the living God of All,
For with them in the furnace he beheld a mighty One,
Whose likeness was the likeness of God's beloved Son.

In the flowery plain of Dura there's no image standing
 now,
And the King of the Chaldeans has no jewels on his
 brow,
For Babylon, the mother of the harlot clothed in red,
For ever has been numbered with the ages that are sped.

THE BEGGARS' BALL.

WHILE mighty things hang in the scales of fate,
And omens black suspicions dark create,
I'll sing of beggars and their ball, I will,
For mad-capp'd rhymers never can be still.

Kind nature, kind to every being, grants
A little bliss to season all their wants ;
John Barleycorn their poverty allayed,
And boist'rous mirth left sorrow in the shade.

The world's a stage, with Shakespeare let me say,
Wherein the poorest have a part to play ;
Round goes the cup that sinks so many low,
And as they quaffed it, drained the deeper woe.

Old hoary veterans, hoary as old time,
Thought they were young, and little past their prime ;
Despotic matrons wore a lively smile,
Such as they wore ere wedlock did them spoil.

The orphan girl and poor neglected boy
Mixed in the dance, and had a taste of joy ;
Dull care for once seemed sunk in Lethé's wave,
And hen-peck'd husbands looked no longer grave.

Oh, glorious ball, thy praise I will resound
From John o' Groat's to earth's remotest bound ;
In their best suits to it they flaunting came,
Nor was an edict passed against the lame.

All were made welcome if they could but crawl
On wooden legs or crutches to the ball ;
The deaf could hear, and palsy got a fright,
And e'en the dumb spoke fluently that night.

And, strange to say, none shades nor patches wore,
Who had so lately eyes both blind and sore ;
Maimed arms and legs no longer could be seen
Until they left next day the festive scene.

Then they appeared as suited best their trade,
All firmly bent upon a begging raid,
Some without stockings, without shirt or shawl,
In quest of alms to make another ball.

A GIPSY SPREE.

In measures full flowing,
The strong ale went round,
And care in the false cup
Of pleasure was drowned.

The bland fragrant zephyrs,
Enchanted, flew by ;
With music and waltzing
There's nothing can vie.

The sons showed the fire
Of their old ancient race ;
The daughters their charms
In the blythe merry pace.

Old feuds were forgot,
And their moments of bliss
Stole softly away
As a warm glowing kiss.

With rude song and riot
The echoes awoke
From the depth of their slumber
In woodland and rock.

Their horses were hoppled,
Escape to prevent,
A bull dog or lurcher
In charge of each tent.

From twilight to dawning
Their mirth never slept,
And to the wild strains
Of the bagpipers leapt.

Their broad swarthy bosoms
With music seemed fired,
And their feet beat the sward
As with rapture inspired.

Such fun and such folly
I ne'er saw before,
And the green flowery lea
Was their carpeted floor.

They drank and caroused
Till the bright stars on high
Were lost in the glory
Of bold Phœbus' eye.

AUTUMN.

THE fair rose fades upon the bush,
Queen Flora with us will not stay,
With summer she will pass away,
And wild winds through the woodlands rush.

The aged earth looks more than fair
For flowers of every hue and gem;
But autumn yet shall blighten them,
And take their fragrance from the air.

His yellow tints are on the leaf
That decks the front of summer's brow;
His breath, I even feel it now,
But with him comes the golden sheaf.

B

The days are turning short again,
The nights are getting drear and long,
And silence steals upon the throng,
Who will not sing beneath his reign.

Yet welcome autumn, laden come,
And fill our stores with thy rich fruit,
Thou source of wealth for man and brute ;
Thrice welcome, though thy looks be glum.

TO A LADY.

OH, lady, how shall I appease
The wrath you vow on me to wreak ?
But why should anger ever tinge
The roses on so fair a cheek ?

If I have hurt one beauteous hair
That flows adown thy swan-like neck,
May summer and her flowerets rare
The plains of Scotia never deck.

If I have hurt your feelings fine,
For truth a martyr I will be ;
So round my neck a strong rope twine,
And drag me to the nearest tree.

For my offence I'll gladly die,
If thou can act the hangman's part ;
But, gracious lady, why deny
And scorn the very thing thou art ?

What though you have no titled name,
I tell you, seriously and frank,
That thou art worthy of the same,
For sterling worth outweigheth rank.

MY WEE LASSIE MARY.

YE winds that o'er the mountains blow,
I charge you wait and carry
A song for me across the sea,
To my sweet lassie Mary,

And tell her that I'm lane without
Her winning laugh and prattle ;
I never see her teething ring,
Her little hose and rattle,

But that the tears come to my e'e,
For weel I lo'ed the fairy ;
And what would I no' gie again
To hae my lassie Mary ?

There's not a flower on summer's plaid
So fair as my wee daughter ;
May every virtue her attend
Ayont the briny water.

So hie away, ye winds that blow,
This song unto her carry,
And bring me back a message frae
My ain wee lassie Mary.

A FAREWELL.

FARE THOU WELL, and tho' we sunder,
Distance cannot true hearts part;
Adieu, adieu, and need we wonder,
Tho' our tears unbidden start.

Here thou art, and where to-morrow,
Far from Hawick, leal and kind;
There's a grandeur in our sorrow,
Such as true hearts only find.

Fare thou well, since fate commands it,
Time's great charger none can stay;
Potentates can not retard it,
And the fates we must obey.

Time may change our frame and faces,
But he cannot change the heart;
Our frail bodies are but cases
That contain the better part.

In our souls true love is woven,
Woven with eternal thread,
Guardian angels, ever rovin'
Round you, wings of glory spread.

Tho' we've been but short together,
We are sad ye're gaun awa,
But, believe us, dearest brother,
After thee our hearts you draw.

THE HAWTHORN TREE.

By the side of Allan water
  There stands a hawthorn tree,
It has seen a thousand summers,
  And has feasted oft the bee.

It has seen a thousand autumns,
  And a thousand merry springs,
And if it had a tongue, 'twould speak
  Of many ancient things.

A thousand times it has been stript,
  And left without a leaf ;
A thousand times it has been deckt
  Gay as an Indian chief.

And many a time the hungry birds
  Have peckt from it the haw,
When other food lay hidden deep
  Beneath the crusted snaw.

As soon as e'er the daisy blooms,
  And nature things renew,
The mavis and her mellow mate
  On it begin to woo.

And round about its time-worn trunk
  Blythe lambs delight to play ;
It has been the pride of Allan
  For a thousand years, they say.

M A Y.

May, with thy dewy lips,
  Kiss me again ;
Row me and trow me
  Once more on the plain.

Welcome, thou cummer,
  Dear to me aye ;
The fairest o' summer
  Is bonnie green May.

The voice o' the cuckoo
  Makes the heart fain ;
O, let me daut thee,
  And ca' you my ain.

Row me and trow me
  Once more in thy dew ;
Month there was never
  So lovely as you.

Row me and trow me
  On yon daisied brae ;
The bride o' the summer
  Is bonnie green May.

D E N H O L M.

The scenes round Denholm, they are rich indeed ;
With Minto hills and crags what can compare ?

And Ruberslaw, whose high majestic head
Towers upward, like the lark, till lost in air ;
And the laburnum, scented sweet, and fair,
Nigh to the parson's mansion may be seen ;
And in memoriam of the poet, see
The people's tribute on the verdant green,
Where sports the bat at eve, at noon the bee,
And youngsters whistling in the leafy dean,
Where the rapt Leyden oft, with ardour keen,
Awoke his lyre with more than master hand :
He has, O Denholm, hallowed here each scene,
And made thee Empress of our Border-land.

THE WOODS.

FRAE this hill tap wi' me look down
    On yonder woods sae bonnie,
For those that skirt the stream o' Jed
    Are fairer far than ony.

The leaves appear as they'd been steept
    In the rich blude o' simmer ;
Nae hand o' airt can imitate
    The hues that deck the timmer.

Wi' them nae rainbow has a share,
    They're busket sae wi' grandeur ;
Ye poets that would have a theme,
    Within those woods but wander.

Though Jed's fair banks be reft o' flowers
　　By Boreas on them blowing,
Wi' me behold the woodlands now,
　　In autumn's glory glowing.

Nae peacock's tail wi' them can vie,
　　Though mooned and unco bonnie,
For those that skirt the stream o' Jed
　　Are fairer far than ony.

MY AULD CLAY BIGGIN.

For six and thirty years I've been
The inmate o' this auld clay biggin,
And though 'tis tenantable yet,
It's turning gey bare o' the riggin.

Like ither cots it e'en maun fail,
A' earthly things are doomed to perish;
And fast the lease is wearin' dune
O' this auld biggin that I cherish.

A new ane, sirs, I'll never need,
And when it lies a wretched ruin
I'll be where flowers celestial bloom,
And wi' bright nymphs rare posies puin'.

Sae o'er my cot I winna mourn,
O' cots like this there's nae repairin';
I ken it's destined to come down,
But let it fa', I am nae carin'.

'Twill serve my turn, I want nae mair,
In it I've had my share o' pleasure,
As well as grief; but of those two,
Of happiness the greatest measure.

So in it I'll contented bide,
Till I be from it ruthless driven;
And when 'tis wrecked by death's strong hand
May I, the inmate, be in heaven.

THE MAIDEN SPRING.

Ho, come with me and greet the spring,
I hear her voice beyond the city,
Dressed in robes of vernal sheen,
Welcome maiden, young and pretty.

Ho, come with me and greet the spring,
And revel in her soft embraces;
We'll meet her on the mountain side,
Where lambkins run their happy races.

Ho, come, make haste and leave the town,
I'm wearied of the smoke and bustle;
I long to hear the song-birds sing,
In woodlands, where the leaflets rustle.

Ho, come with me and greet the spring,
Through fairy bowers the winds are sighing;
And round about the farmer's home,
Behold the little swallows flying.

Ho, come with me and greet the spring,
Her hands are full of sweetest posies ;
A crown of sunbeams on her head,
And bosom braided o'er with roses.

Ho, come with me, ye pent-up souls,
And view the maiden that is smiling ;
Beyond the town there's blooming flowers,
And busy bees upon them toiling.

The tyrant winter now is dead,
And for him we've no tears of pity ;
Clap hands, and shout, for, lo, I hear
The maiden spring approach the city.

D E L I A.

HOLD to mine eye that glass through which I see
No other object than the face of thee,
The first of flowers and pride of woman kind,
Your Samson I, with slender threads me bind.

Can heaven above a fairer angel show
Than thou, my Delia, fairest here below ?
How dim the blue of bright Italian skies
Compared to thy angelic, dreamy eyes.

Oh, let me feast till wearied on those lips,
Sweeter than aught the bee from blossom sips ;
Your breast the snow untrampled in the glade,
Thy cheeks carnations in full beauty spread.

No ideal fiction thou, created in the brain
Of some crazed poet—few of them are sane ;
No, thou art real, and living upon earth,
Of heavenly mould, though but of mortal birth.

No Grecian maid in charms with thee can vie,
Your image haunts me, and seems ever nigh ;
Where'er I muse, where'er I chance to stray,
Thy beauteous form still meets me in the way.

THE LARK.

HIGH o'er the shepherd's cot,
Lilting a cheery note,
Bird of the moorland,
   I wish I were thee.
Up in that azure home,
Angels and spirits roam ;
And had I but pinions,
   Up there I would be.

Up in the boundless sky,
Lost to the human eye,
Bird of the moorland,
   With dew-dripping breast ;
High o'er the flowery lawn,
Hailing the rosy dawn,
Warbling thy sweet strains,
   The wildest and best.

High o'er the snowy cloud,
White as the whitest shroud,
Bird of the moorland,
    And herald of day ;
Up 'mid the golden stars,
O'er the horizon bars,
At heaven's gate singing
    A heart-stirring lay.

THE SOUL.

MYSTERIOUS thing, beyond all finding out,
Clothed with belief and swaddled up in doubt,
Ah, what art thou ?   We say the thinking part,
Thy seat, where is it, in the head or heart ?

The head, if injured, reason goes astray,
And canst thou think when severed from the clay ;
I muse on thee till all my senses swim,
Why clear just now, and why next moment dim ?

No atheist I ; Almighty God forbid,
Though I would know what Thou hast from me hid ;
In chaos, gropping with a wavering mind,
Perplexed and puzzled with myself and kind.

O God, I own Thee as the ruling power
Whose word created man, beast, bird, and flower ;
Thy works delight me wheresoe'er I gaze,
And all my being teems with love and praise.

And reason tells me man is far above
All creatures here in anger or in love ;
Brutes have their passions, instinct them controls,
And men have these, and they have also souls.

But what's the soul ?   I cannot comprehend,
And there be none who can assistance lend ;
My finite sense confounds me every way,
Yet there is something, be whate'er it may.

In vain the search ; for man can never know
That precious gem designed for weal or woe,
Till past the threshold ; why, then, struggle here ?
The day's not distant when it shall be clear.

GOD IS HERE.

YES, God is here ; His greatness I can trace
On all I see in this wild desert place ;
Those rugged rocks attest His awful power,
These blades of grass, and, lo, that tiny flower.

One feeds my flocks, the other feasts the bee,
The winds and waters speak of Him to me ;
And that blythe bird, the lark, delights mine ear ;
Though in the wilds, I cannot weary here.

Rich scented zephyrs round about me stray,
And snow-white lambkins, sportive, leap and play.
Yes, God is here all nature doth declare,
Those plains and mountains testimony bear.

The tides of joy I feel within my soul,
Like waves of ocean through me surge and roll;
How sweet the blackbird sings on yonder tree;
Though in the wilds, His glory I can see.

Ye butterflies that trip so gay along,
Flaunt into verse and beautify my song;
And you, ye rills, which meander calm and clear,
In heavenly language tell me God is here.

I feel enraptured, and I more than feel
A hallowed transport o'er my being steal;
What lovely flowers, all beauty, I behold,
Some white, some crimson, others like pure gold.

They glad my heart, and all my cares beguile,
And as I look on them they seem to smile.
Yes, God is here, though but a desert place;
On all I see His finger-prints can trace.

SEPTEMBER.

The laverock, it has left the sky,
In flocks the birds together fly,
Our simmer days they'll sune be by,
    So let us hail September.

Bland zephyrs drink the sweet perfume
Of heather, a' in purple bloom;
And richly-laden bees hie home
    Wi' treasure in September.

Out on the moors, 'mid heath and ling,
The bick'ring grouse, the pointer's spring,
And deadly guns make echoes ring
   Wi' volleys in September.

Look down the strath on harvest rig,
See lads and lassies neat and trig,
And sober matrons fat and big,
   Right merry in September.

Like trainéd soldiers, stooks o' grain
Stand at attention on the plain,
And signs o' plenty maketh fain
   The farmers in September.

Though blighted now the briar rose,
Red cheeket apples bend the boughs,
Hazel nuts and jet-black sloes
   Are smiling in September.

What though our birds of song are mute,
The glorious autumn brings us fruit,
And wi' poetic pride I'll tout
   The praises o' September.

Of a' the months that's in the year,
There's nane sae fraught as it wi' cheer;
And to our hearts there's none so dear
   As couthie, kind September.

DEPARTED MAID.

Departed maid, with grief I sing
A dirge above thy early bier;
Flowers die in autumn, bloom in spring,
But thy cold urn no spring can cheer.

Methinks I see you, even now,
As fresh and rosy as before;
Thy sparkling eyes and Grecian brow,
Alas! dear maid, I'll view no more.

But yesterday I saw thee bloom,
And far the spoiler seemed from thee;
The grave, it may thy form consume,
But there thy spirit cannot be.

Now far above this world of care,
With kindred spirits dost thou roam:
Ah, yes! I fancy thou art there,
With Him who made not earth His home.

Then fare you well, though weak the rhyme,
No other tribute can I pay
To thee, within that blissful clime,
Where suns set not, nor skies turn grey.

Though fancy thus unveils to me
The noble form which erst thou wore;
But stript of it, what must thou be?
The fairest on that far-off shore.

Departed maid, with grief I sing,
And weep above thy early bier ;
Flowers die in autumn, bloom in spring,
But thy cold urn no spring can cheer.

TAKE FROM MINE EYES.

TAKE from mine eyes the misty veil of sin,
And light the clearest on my soul let in ;
Dispel the darkness of my clouded mind,
Thou who, at cool Siloam, cured the blind.

Take from my hands those chains by Satan made,
And with Thy light my being Thou pervade ;
And like the beggar whom Thou didst restore
To brilliant day, mine eyes, like his, rub o'er.

Thy light withhold not, let me feel the rays
Stream on mine eyelids in a perfect blaze ;
Write on my heart the dictates of Thy will :
My darkened soul with light eternal fill.

Oh, take from me the vicious love of sin :
Here let me wash my guilty soul within
The precious blood which from Thy side did flow ;
In garments clothe me whiter than the snow.

C

THE SNOWDROPS.

PRECURSORS o' simmer,
Through the snaw glimmer,
Come in your white robes, glad us again ;
Come in your virgin pride,
Smile on the Teviotside,
Long in the woodlands of Branxholm remain.

There, where the lilies fair
Hang out their dresses rare,
There where the song-birds their sweet ditties sing ;
High on the budding trees,
Rocked by the balmy breeze,
Hailing with rapture the birth o' the spring.

Fierce winter is waning,
And young spring is dawning,
Though distant, I hear the sweet sound o' her feet ;
With flowers she is laden,
The pure, spotless maiden
Has made all the pulses of nature to beat.

The winter is dreary,
For simmer I weary,
The snowdrops they tell us of winter's decay ;
He's dying, he's dying,
The wild winds are sighing,
And all God's creation seems tired o' his sway.

Hail to the merry spring,
Mount up, ye larks, and sing,
Why are ye silent, ye masters of song?
Heed not the blinding sleet,
Warble in ether sweet,
Wake up, thou mavis, why slumber so long?

Mourn not o'er winter's bier,
Spring comes with gladsome cheer,
Pregnant is earth with her millions of flowers.
Through the snaw glimmer,
Ye heralds o' simmer,
Usher the spring into this land of ours.

W I N T E R.

Ay, this is winter, and the tyrant reigns
As mighty monarch never reigned before;
The murmuring brooks are bound with crystal chains,
And sweet-voiced songsters gather round the door.

Upon the banks of yonder glassy stream,
Age, staff in hand, admires the pranks of youth—
Of early days there let him muse and dream,
For they are fled, and age is full of ruth.

Fain would he throw his age and staff away,
And mingle with those children full of fun;
'Tis vain the wish, for he is old and grey,
And from his glass of life the sand has run.

The eternal round of seasons smiteth man,
And leaveth deep impressions on his brow ;
But yesterday, methinks, he jumped and ran,
The same as any of those children now.

But he has had his day, and youth can have no more,
The world itself remaineth not aye green ;
The locks of twenty soon get silvered o'er,
And snowy age becomes a winter scene.

On ice transparent as the clearest glass,
With skate-clad feet the skaters move along ;
With them how light the frosty minutes pass,
For winter cannot harm the young and strong.

Fair damsels, fair as summer's fairest rose,
Hie from the city to the amber streams ;
And when the short-lived day draws to a close,
Of victories unwon the curler dreams.

Oh, savage winter, with your stormy skies,
Upon the poor ye grievous burdens throw ;
Yet to the rich ye bring rare exercise,
Who, with their steeds and sledges, love the snow.

The farmers ye have smitten hip and thigh,
Snow on uplands never lay so deep,
And all the land rings with a doleful cry
Of tenderest pity for the starving sheep.

The sheep may hungry be upon the hills,
But lower down, in many a humble cot,

The hand of poverty imposeth ills
Of which few heed or even taketh note.

Oh, winter, winter ! cruel-hearted king,
With sceptre such as monarch never swayed ;
From man and beast ye countless comforts wring,
By mandates that must be by all obeyed.

But this, remember, you shall from us pass,
When joyous spring re-robes the earth in green ;
We'll then forget your stern, despotic laws,
And glory in you hustled off the scene.

YOUNG YEAR'S DAY.

Wi' tears, cauld tears, upon its cheek,
   The young year came in sighin' ;
The streets wi' folk were mair than thrang,
   Some singin' and some cryin',
     On Young Year's Day.

Frae house to house first-fitters went,
   And even bonnie lasses
Thought it nae ill to welcome them
   And pree their reamin' glasses
     On Young Year's Day.

Auld crazy sires, wi' hair like snaw,
   Sat near the reekin' toddy,

And had their crack and 'bacca blaw
   Like ony 'ither body
     On Young Year's Day.

And couthie, kindly, auld grand dames
   Had on their bràwest mutches ;
And weary, wand'ring, mortal mèn
   Felt glad upon their crutches
     On Young Year's Day.

The bairnies, too—God bless them a'—
   Had a' things worth the eatin' ;
And mither's got nae broos to kiss,
   For nane o' them were greetin'
     On Young Year's Day ;

For a' were crouse, and revelled in
   The cosy lap o' nature,
And soothin' Bliss out-stretch'd her wings,
   And happit every creature
     On Young Year's Day.

T E A R S.

THE purest tears that ever were shed,
Are those which fall by the sacred dead ;
To-day, by the grave of one laid low,
I saw them trickle, I watched them flow.

And, like gems, they shone on the coffin lid,
Sad heralds of thoughts in the bosom hid ;
They melted my heart, and this you'll own,
That tears, like rain, can moisten stone.

In the hour of grief, by the sacred dead,
Oh, there's nought so pure as the tears we shed ;
Let fame, proud fame, her proud statues rear
Above her sons, but give me a tear.

Oh, give me a tear, and give me a sigh,
When under the sod I am doomed to lie ;
I would rather have these direct from the heart,
Than a sculptured stone from the hand of art.

Oh, what can compare with the tears that are shed
By sorrowing friends o'er the graves of their dead ;
There is something about them akin to divine,
On the robes of the dead how they sparkle and shine.

Brighter than pearls by our Indians worn,
And pure as the dew of the virgin morn ;
When lowly laid, and consigned to my bier,
Oh, give me a sigh, and give me a tear.

In the hour of death it has oft been said
That angels, unseen, around us tread ;
And for aught that I know, away they may bear,
On the tips of their wings, to heaven a tear ;

For there's nought so pure as the tears we shed
Above the white shrouds of the sacred dead;
They come from our heart, and roll from the eye,
Like emeralds dropt by the seraphs on high.

When around the grave of some dear one dead,
Oh, there's nought so pure as the tears we shed;
I watched them to-day, in a hallowed place,
In their purity steal o'er many a face:

Round, big, and clear as the dewdrops at May,
Which shimmer and shine on the leafy spray;
They melted my heart, and this you'll own,
That tears, like rain, can moisten stone.

THE GREEN HILLSIDE.

Oh, come with me, the city leave,
And let us rove on yon hillside,
Where happy children chaplets weave
With flowerets in their bloomy pride.

Within the town I cannot stay;
I'm wearied of the struggling scene,
The clank of labour night and day,
Without one quiet hour between.

Then with me to the mountains haste,
And snuff awhile the caller air;
With toil incessant never waste
The forms which all too quickly wear.

Upon the hills we'll pleasure find
Such as no town can to us give ;
And solitude uplifts the mind
To Him who once on earth did live.

All things around us here convey
Unto our ears the voice of God ;
He speaks to us in many a way,
And decks with flowers the desert road.

Within the town I cannot trace
The foot-prints of the Mighty One
Who lifted darkness off the face
Of nature, and gave us that sun ;

Now shining in the heavens high,
What hand directs or doth it guide ?
The very zephyrs make reply,
'Tis He who paints the green hillside.

THE PRIDE O' TEVIOT.

WITH trembling lips I now essay
To sing of one, the pride of Teviot ;
'Twould take a Byron to portray
Charms such as her's, you may believe it.

She is no common, ideal maid,
Her bright blue eyes and golden tresses
A heavy tax on me have laid,
And for a song the poet presses.

Before me, now, she seems to stand
The heroine of this epistle;
The slightest touch of her white hand
Would make the saddest poet whistle.

Her form is slender, tall, and straight
As any tassled blooming willow;
My aching head, I fain would lay it
Upon her breast, a pleasant pillow.

Her lips the red rose petals fair,
With love's sweet dew upon them lying;
To sip it many venture there,
But all must yield to her denying.

Oh, what would I not give to win
The heart of such a peerless maiden;
With rosy cheeks and dimpled chin,
And, more than all, with graces laden.

Though oft I have entangled been
Within the net of love's strange meshes,
I never spied a fairer queen—
Her very look my soul refreshes.

MY DARLING MAID.

My darling maid, nipp'd in the bud,
  What fond hearts o'er thee mourn;
The nest that charmed a happy pair
  Is rifled now and torn.

Ah ! who can feign a father's grief,
  Or like a mother feel,
When death has spread his gloomy pall
  Around us like a veil ?

Where is the maid I used to meet
  Sae blythe, where Bowmont rows
Its sparkling waters to the Till,
  By Clifton's broomy knowes ?
I need not ask ; this lint-white lock,
  Bound with a silken thread,.
Proclaims the truth in language plain,
  My darling maid is dead.

With syren tongue she won my heart,
  When sitting on my knee ;
Would twine her arms about my neck,
  And tell her 'plaints to me.
The kisses that I then received
  From her I'll ne'er forget
Until my latest sun sinks down,
  In death for ever set.

Life at the best is but a gift,
  And He who it bestows
Has measured out with mighty hand
  The time when it shall close.
Her hour was come, no longer here
  Could my sweet darling stay ;
And like a rosebud newly blown,
  Was blasted in a day.

O God, impart to all a balm
  With downcast stricken soul ;
Dry up the fount from whence the tears
  Of anguish rapid roll.
Ye parent pair, though wrung with grief,
  And rifled be your nest ;
Oh, learn to say, " Thy will be done,"
  For surely He knows best.

For earth He saw she was too fair,
  And gave her to His Son,
Who, with His blood on Calvary,
  Your little darling won.
Now in His home, where sapphires blaze,
  And rainbow colours glow ;
She wears a crown which ne'er a queen
  Nor king ere wore below.

NO MORE OF YOUR BELLES.

No more of your belles, be they dark-eyed or not,
Like a child with its toys, of them I am tired ;
My bosom with rapture responds to them not,
And fled are the sweet nymphs that once me inspired.

Like a steed in my youth, unaccustomed to reins,
I roved through the mazes of pleasure at will ;
My cup it was sweet, and though still it remains,
My ardour is gone, and my heart waxes chill.

I have seen, when an eye full of language and love,
In the head of some Delia could thrill me all o'er ;
But now I am changed, and no eyes can me move,
Be they black, blue, or grey, as they charmed me before.

At the fountain of folly I've drunk till I'm sick,
In search now of wisdom the world I'll explore ;
But where shall I find it ? Ye sages, come, speak,
Since those angelic creatures delight me no more.

When the cranium turns bare, and age wrinkles the brow,
It is time—is it not ?—after wisdom to seek ;
Oh, had I been wise, and sage as I'm now,
No traces of riot had been on my cheek.

Draw near, thou young stripling, of summers sixteen,
And hear what the senior of twice that can say ;
When I was a youngster, just like thee, I ween,
On foibles I squandered my spring-time away.

O'er time that I've wasted, how oft do I grieve ;
In vain do I murmur—in vain do I sigh ;
For years that are gone, could I but retrieve,
How different, how different I would them apply.

THE HEID.

BAIRNIES wi' it get sic frichts,
There's no ane that sleeps soun' ;
Oh ! the heid, the horrid heid,
What brought it to the toon ?

It rows aboot, it trows aboot,
Baith near and far awa';
Whiles it is on the Maiden's Paps,
And whiles on Ruberslaw.

It rows aboot, it trows aboot,
The like o't ne'er was seen ;
The ither nicht it lichted up
The hale o' Denholm Dean.

Oh ! the heid, the fearsome heid,
That rows aboot at nicht ;
There's no a bairnic dare gae oot,
Unless that it be licht.

It rows aboot, it trows aboot,
There ne'er was sic a heid ;
I wonder if phrenologists
The bumps o' it could read.

It gliffs the auld, it gliffs the young,
And, certes, 'tis nae freak ;
At dark midnicht, on passers-by,
'Twill through the hedgerows keek.

Oh ! the heid, the weird-like heid,
It's like nane ever saw ;
I wonder if it e'er was worn
By onie ane ava.

But to the story that's afloat,
I'll tell it while 'tis green :
Near Goldielands, within the wood,
A heidless man was seen.   .

It rows aboot, it trows aboot,
And they who saw him fled,
Declare he was no other than
The owner o' this head.

A LUMP IN THE THROAT.

MANKIND at the best are but a funny lot,
    But the queerest o' mortals that ever was seen
Was a gaucy auld wife wi' a lump in her throat,
    And hoo it was taen oot ye'll no guess, I ween.

Her throat it was a' richt, but then, dae ye see,
    The cranium was saft, and her mind was a' gyte ;
She naething could swallow, not e'en a drap tea,
    Sae aff to the doctor she went in a plight.

She came to his mansion, and tugged at the bell,
    The servant it answered, then said the auld dame—
" Giff he's in, will ye tell him it's Betsy hersel';"
    " Hech, now, but I'm pleased to hear he's at hame."

" This way," said the doctor ; " here, Betsy, sit doon,"
    And rolled up the sleeves o' his braw glossy coat ;

" I'll bet you," quoth he, " frae a bob to a croon,
　　That I'll sune take that big lump frae oot o' yere
　　　　throat."

Sae he fingered awa' at her weezen a while,
　　And then he performed a wizard-like feat ;
O' instruments, he frae a case took a pile,
　　And wi' ane, like a whaup's neb, he nailed it complete.

" Shut your eyes, and gape wide." · Sae the auld bodie
　　　　gapt
　　Jist like a young craw when receivin' its food ;
In her throat, wi' a pair o' lang plyers, he scrapt,
　　But the canty auld beldame the whole affair stood.

He feigned fairly baffled, but after a rest
　　Of a minute or so he tried it again ;
A bit o' bees'-wax in the pincers he put,
　　Then, astonished, showed Betsy the lump he had
　　　　taen

Frae out o' her throat.　Had ye seen hoo she stared,
　　For it maist was the size o' a cushie doo's egg ;
She threw doon a guinea, and thought it weel waired,
　　For he, to her ailment, had given a fleg.

The guinea the doctor gave her it again,
　　And rolled down the sleeves o' his good glossy coat ;
The auld gratefu' creature, she thanked him amain,
　　And hame she returned wi' nae lump in her throat.

'TWILL SUNE BE WINTER NOO.

DARK, stormy clouds bedim the skies
    That were in summer blue ;
And a' the hills wi' snaw are white—
    'Twill sune be winter noo.

Within the forest Boreas wails,
    And lifts on high the leaves ;
Though sharp and chill his boist'rous breath,
    It dries the dripping sheaves.

I feel the hand of winter cauld
    Upon my cheek and broo ;
Of a' their pride the woods are shorn—
    'Twill sune be winter noo.

The lang clear days o' simmer shine
    Again hae fleeted by ;
And a' the flowers o' sweetest bloom
    In direst ruin lie.

Adown the vale by autumn sered,
    Nae mair the cushats coo ;
And a' the birds of song are mute—
    'Twill sune be winter noo.

The glory o' the autumn's gone,
    And winter's speeding back ;
His stormy clouds the hill-tops hide
    Wi' pinions broad and black.

D

It makes me wae when winter treads
    The woodlands through and through ;
In nature's hand a withered bough—
    'Twill sune be winter noo.

THE CREATOR.

THE power of our Mighty Creator
    On all things around me I see ;
E'en the touch of His finger reviveth
    Ilk blighted and bare-looking tree.

Now straight from His hand comes the summer,
    With daisies in bloom 'neath her feet ;
And nature, so chilled by the winter,
    Feels the heart in her great bosom beat.

On nature we look, and we wonder
    At the power of that Spirit Divine,
Whose voice is the loud-rolling thunder,
    His glory the lightnings that shine,

His chariot the fast-flying tempest,
    His pathway the deep, restless main ;
And, lo, on the tips of his fingers
    The out and the in pulling rein.

He guides and directs as He pleases,
    This world and the creatures He made ;
And summer, with soft-scented breezes,
    He sendeth once more to the glade.

Her herald, the cuckoo, I hear it
   Proclaiming her march o'er the land,
The signet of God, yes, I see it,
   On all things the work of His hand.

WHAT IS MAN?

Oh, what is man?   A little dust
In balance hanging, rarely just,
    And prone to err ;
Yes, we are frail, and apt to fall
Low as the lowest brutes of all,
    Down in the mire.

We rise to-day, to-morrow fa',
O'er those that's doon we need not craw
    Wi' souls elate ;
For who can tell how sune we may
Be lower sunken still than they,
    The sport of fate.

When mortals off the high-road gang,
They stumble on, and soon get wrang,
    In gutter or in ditch.
Life's wee short path is rough and slid,
And fu' o' dangers frae us hid,
    That oft us backward pitch.

Like leaves in autumn hither toss'd,
We whirl about on life's strange coast,
    And oft without a freen ;

Queer pranks the fates on mankind play,
And unco little down can lay
      The best of us, I ween.

Sae pity those that step aside,
Ye that are wise the foolish guide,
      And help them if ye can ;
'Tis human nature to transgress ;
If angels fell, then wonder less
      At woman or at man,

Who may be subject to the power
Of Satan in an evil hour,
      'Tis easy to get wrang ;
And when we tumble in the glaur
There's plenty aye to make it waur,
      But few to soothe a pang.

THE HEART.

CAN the heart love at sixty the same as sixteen ?
To this, what's the answer ?   A loud ringing " No ;"
The leaves o' last summer shall never be green ;
And the heart that is withered can never be so.

At sixty the rapture of eighteen has fled,
While the red stream of life in the veins circle cold;
The feelings of twenty at threescore are dead,
And the bright eye gets dim as the heart waxeth old.

Dare Cupid at sixty awake in the breast
The wild burning passions of sweet twenty-one ?
Shall the bird back with ardour return to its nest,
When the season of hatching and rearing is done ?

Shall the dark eyes of Delia rekindle again
The embers she kindled in days long ago ?
As well seek for roses in bloom on the plain,
In the depth of December, amid the chill snow.

Ah, no ! it is folly thus ever to dream,
For youth is the season of vigour and fire ;
Though the shafts of wee Cupid still pointed may seem,
To the altar at sixty—ah ! never aspire.

THE AUTUMN LEAF.

I NEVER see an autumn leaf
    But what I think upon
The days of youth, for ever sped,
    And old age coming on.

It seemeth not long since I was
    A little puny boy,
Climbing on my father's knee,
    So full of mirth and joy.

But, ah ! reality, though stern,
    Her finger points to truth ;
Those days are gone, and, like this leaf,
    I've lost the hue of youth.

Had I but better spent those days,
   Then less I would regret ;
But conscious that I used them ill,
   I cannot help but fret.

Within this blighted leaf I see
   More than I can explain ;
When withered thus, ah ! what can make
   The bosom green again.

My youth is past, I see the tint
   Of autumn's fierce career ;
Upon my cheeks and on my brow
   His ravages appear.

Time steals away, I can't tell how—
   The days of men are brief ;
And youth might well a lesson take
   From this, an autumn leaf.

NAE FLOWERS IN WINTER.

THEY'RE nae flowers in winter,
   And bare ilka tree ;
O, haste back, sweet summer,
   Bring roses to me ;
Bring leaves green and dewy
   To garnish the thorn,
And laden with perfume
   The wings o' the morn.

O come wi' soft breezes,
   Re-daisy the lea ;
Oh, haste back, sweet summer,
   Wi' roses to me :
Bring wallflowers, sweet-williams,
   And sweet mignonette,
And other braw flowerets
   Whose names I forget.

I likena the winter,
   Sae cauld aye is he ;
Oh, haste back, sweet summer,
   Wi' roses to me :
Bring violets and pansies,
   And carnations fair,
The crocus and lily
   Sae modest and rare.

Now hushed in the woodlands
   The mavis's glee ;
Oh, haste back, sweet summer,
   Wi' roses to me.
I long for the flowerets
   And hum o' the bee ;
Oh, hasten, sweet summer,
   Bring roses to me.

SPRING.

Come to us in robes of splendour,
   Wove in mighty nature's loom ;

Come with leaflets green and tender,
　Gowans white and yellow broom.

Come with long days calm and sunny,
　Merry evenings short and sweet ;
Come with lambkins blythe and funny,
　Sporting in old Phœbus' heat.

Come with sunshine, bees, and flowers,
　We have waited for you long ;
Renovate the blighted bowers,
　Make the woodlands ring with song.

Come with dewdrops clear and pearly,
　Shining in your locks so fair ;
Come, sweet maiden, and come early,
　Bid us not of thee despair.

Come, fair maid, in robes of grandeur,
　Hasten back to us in bloom ;
Dewy flowers the rarest squander
　Lavishly on winter's tomb.

THE GOWANS.

They beautify our Border hills,
　Like stars bestud the valleys,
Amongst them sports the butterfly,
　And o'er them skim the swallows.

I mind it well, when I was young,
   A romping, tricky shaver,
I used to cull the gowans white,
   And wi' them busk my beaver.

I wish I were a child again,
   For manhood's such a battle ;
Now, like a cart on a rough road,
   Amid the ruts I rattle.

How happy when I was a child,
   Amid the moors and mosses ;
A stranger to the ways of men,
   And life wi' a' its crosses.

And though those days have passed away
   Like dreams I've had in slumber,
The gowans still as pretty grow,
   And who could here them number.

THE SNOWDROPS.

O WELCOME back, in spotless dress,
Ye messengers of spring, so fair :
Exposed to February air,
Your mission is not ill to guess ;

For you are come to let us know
That vernal spring will soon be here ;
The tidings must all mankind cheer,
For we are tired of frost and snow.

And you are welcome to the glade,
The fairest in our Border land ;
For there's no place like Teviot's strand,
On which the winter's made a raid.

At your approach with pain he sighs,
With grief his icy hands doth wring ;
He dreads the touch of gentle spring,
For at her touch the monarch dies.

His strength is ebbing fast away,
He hates the look of you, all bloom ;
His wrathful eyes are full of gloom,
The sceptre long he cannot sway.

Then, welcome back, ye tiny flowers,
In robes the purest ever worn :
To winter spread them out with scorn,
Your smile the tyrant overpowers.

He's dying fast, he's dying fast ;
Ye messengers of early spring,
Your praise a thousand minstrels sing,
Though ye but bloom to die at last.

A HARVEST PRAYER.

Thou great mysterious Power on high,
Whom all that breathe on earth revere ;
The prayers of Thy servants hear,
And send us weather clear and dry.

The dripping clouds rebottle up,
And give the reapers strength to reap
The food of oxen and of sheep,
And fill, O Lord, the poor man's cup.

Shield Thou the plenteous crops from rain ;
How fair the yellow corn-fields glow,
The wealth of autumn bends the bough ;
O Lord, the elements restrain.

Bid Thou the clouds withhold their tears,
More than enough they've wept of late ;
While weary farmers watch and wait,
And forward look to better years.

Our fields demand the sickles now,
To Phœbus give a brighter eye ;
For bread may no poor orphans cry ;
To harvest give a shining brow.

Then let us toil with hope and cheer,
And gather in the fruits of earth ;
For plenty makes a happy hearth,
And none but sluggards want need fear.

Preserve, O Lord, the golden feast,
Upon Thy goodness all depend ;
This weather change, and better send,
To glad the heart of man and beast.

THE FLOWERS O' SPRING.

THE crocuses and snowdrops white,
They are, indeed, the flowers o' spring ;
And budding woods with love-notes ring,
For winter's wearing out of sight.

Above the sky is clear and blue,
No dark clouds float across the scene ;
For spring's returning back, I ween,
The face of nature to renew.

For crocuses and snowdrops white,
Within our gardens neat and trim,
Display the wondrous power o' Him
Whose word created day and night.

Fair emblems of man's sinless state,
With tints of heaven in their eyes,
From out the earth they upward rise
To welcome back the spring elate.

Before our days of death and pain,
In Eden could they fairer be ?
But Adam ate from off the tree,
Which did the whole creation stain.

And can it be that sin would taint
The very flowers when mankind fell ;
And would they have a sweeter smell,
Or hues which none need hope to paint ?

It matters not what they were then,
Their charms are quite sufficient now
To deck the front of nature's brow,
And beautify the homes of men.

On many a little grassy mound,
Above the dust of dear ones dead,
A soothing influence they shed
On hearts with sorrow almost drowned.

Oh, pluck them not, but let them blow,
For, like ourselves, they onward pass :
Too soon they'll sink beneath the grass,
And others in their places grow.

THE HEDGEROWS.

THE fair hedgerows are wet with dew,
Athwart the hills the flocks are spread,
And briar roses, white and red,
Among the hawthorns peeping through.

Like Eastern maidens, thickly veiled
From all the sons of mortal clay,
They blossom by the rough pathway,
And charm us though they be concealed.

Now piping loud as loud can be,
The merry lark in ether clear ;
In yon hay fields the craiks I hear,
And all the woods are full of glee.

Hail, summer ; hail the gowans white,
With their sweet faces deck the brae ;
In scented swathes the fragrant hay
Perfumes the dewy robes of night.

When eve let's down her starry screen,
No grander scene could be than this ;
For lover's walk and lover's kiss
Betwixt the hedgerows fresh and green.

A WEE SWEET FLOWER.

A WEE sweet flower, just opening out,
    Within the dust lies blighted ;
Forgive those tears which stain the sheet,
    For I can scarcely write it.

Without it bare the garden seems,
    For fondly on't we lookit ;
But death came by, and, lo, the flower
    Away with him he took it :

For heaven willed it should be ta'en,
    And though we wished to keep it,
We know 'tis safe with Him who once
    Within a manger sleepit.

'Twas only lent us for a while,
    To fill our hearts with gladness ;
But even in the train of bliss
    There comes a flood of sadness.

Through tears of grief we saw it fade,
    And from us ever riven ;
'Tis hard to say, " Thy will be done,"
    But yield we must to heaven.

And there it blooms a fairer flower,
    Within an endless morrow,
And nestling in the breast of Him
    Who had on earth His sorrow.

THE QUEEN OF MAY.

BATHED and refreshed by April's showers,
The beauteous May to us has come ;
Her leafy locks are full of flowers,
On which the wild bees feast and hum.

'Tis summer now, and all the woods
Are dressed in garments green and gay ;
And winter, with his leaden clouds,
Has died within the arms of May.

And he has passed from off the earth,
The same as if he ne'er had been ;
And kindly nature's given birth
Unto another sweet May Queen.

With Phœbus up our daughters rose,
And hastened forth from out the town ;
The dew of May they would not lose,
And in it bathed on yonder down,

Where they poured out their hearts in song,
And plaited gowans in their hair;
For May with sweets detained them long,
And with them gamboled here and there.

A fairer queen none ever met,
Upon her head a crown of flowers,
With silvery dewdrops dripping wet,
Out walking in the morning hours.

The birds her greeted on the trees,
The lambkins in her lap did play;
And zephyrs came frae yont the seas
To kiss the cheek of pretty May.

THE SWALLOWS.

Oh, come back, ye swallows,
  Come over the main;
Return to my cottage,
  And twitter again.
I'm tired o' the winter,
  Sae cauld aye is he;
Oh, come on swift pinions
  Wi' summer to me.

Oh, come back, ye swallows,
  You're dear to my heart;
Return to my cottage,
  And round the eaves dart.

I like nae the winter,
  Sae cauld aye is he ;
Oh, come on swift pinions,
  Wi' summer to me.

Oh, come back, ye swallows,
  Wi' summer return ;
I wish that the winter
  Were laid in his urn,
And saw you swift darting
  O'er meadow and lea ;
Oh, haste back, ye swallows,
  Wi' summer to me.

JOCKIE.

JOCKIE sware by a' the stars
In that blue sky above me,
And I, like any simple maid,
Believed he truly loved me.

But men, I trow, are fickle as
The clouds that float on high ;
He's woo'd and won another maid,
  And me he passes by.

But let him go, I do not care,
I've got as braw a chiel,
And ane that nae daft glaiket jade
Dare ever frae me steal.

E

In wedlock's net I hae him fast,
And round his neck a noose
That his twa hands can ne'er untie,
And none but death it loose.

And there I'll keep him—yes, I will—
And by those stars above me ;
And by this earth and a' therein
I ken he truly loves me.

S U M M E R.

THE summer's come, like maiden young and gay,
And with her tresses fragrant zephyrs play ;
Her handmaid Flora welcomes forth the bee,
And butterflies are sporting o'er the lea.

On all around the finger-prints of God,
With fairest blossom orchards now are load ;
High overhead the lark's delightful strain
Charms the lone heart of many a toiling swain.

With sweetest song the minstrels charm the glade,
And stretcht at ease the shepherd in his plaid ;
His faithful dogs lie basking in the heat,
One at his head, the other at his feet.

Wide o'er the hill his flock content are spread,
Below the swallows twitter round the shed ;
And in the vale, on pasture rich and green,
The useful cows, with udders full, are seen.

No more the woods look cheerless, bare, and bleak,
For summer reigns with roses on her cheek;
No human hand her garments wove in loom,
Queen of the year, attired in rarest bloom.

At her approach all nature rises up,
And sweets again refill the poet's cup;
No more dare winter show his scowling face,
He's dead and buried in some secret place.

The leafy summer, fairest without spot,
Her vestures seem as if by angels wrought;
The dews of eve refresh her painted flowers,
And clouds them water with reviving showers.

Her herald, the cuckoo, lilts the whole day long,
And loud the landrail craiks the hay among;
O'er hawthorn bloom how blythe the wild bees hum,
And feast upon the sweets of summer come.

WEE WILLIE.

Scarce nine months old when he was snatcht,
  Like flower in sweetest blossom,
And little did we ever think
  That we were doomed to lose him.

The wee sweet flower, we watched it bud,
  Nor dreamed that death sae chilly
Would come sae soon, and take away
  Our Willie, wee sweet Willie.

Abune him noo the sods are spread,
  And sered leaves on them lyin';
And many a time when nane me see,
  In sorrow wrapt sit cryin'.

Upon the stars enrapt I gaze,
  In evenings dark and stilly;
And there I feast my longing eyes
  Wi' looking up to Willie.

A better child I never saw,
  Sae easy pleased and canny;
And unco lane are we without
  Our Willie, puir wee manny.

His ring and rattle to me speak,
  And when I'm busy toilin',
Within the empty cradle oft
  Methinks I see him smilin'.

'Tis hard to part wi' those we love,
  And though our hearts be riven,
We know he's safe in Christ on high,
  And him we'll meet in heaven.

DAUGHTER OF BABYLON.

COME down, fair daughter, low, and sit down in the
  very dust,
The golden sceptre from thy hand shall be for ever thrust;

The royal crown which decks thy head, asunder shall
 be rent ;
Come down, fair daughter, from thy throne, in ashes
 thou lament.

Take thou the millstones, and grind meal, with limbs
 and bosom bare ;
The bracelets take off thy white arms, the fillets out
 your hair ;
Aside the sparkling jewels put, thy silken robes gae
 fauld,
For lady of the kingdoms thou shall never more be
 called.

And you have said that thou wouldst be a lady ever
 gay,
Oh, daughter of Chaldeans, mourn in widowhood
 array,
For all the things have come to pass which thou thoughtst
 distant far ;
Upon thy brow no diamonds shine, and on thy breast
 no star.

Enchantments are of no avail, and sorceries are vain ;
No rings upon thy fingers blaze, around thy neck no
 chain ;
Of all thy grandeur thou'st been reft—of it stript in an
 hour ;
Oh, daughter of the Chaldeans, mourn, thy cup is more
 than sour.

Thy throne, fair daughter, where is't now? and where
    the envied crown?
The tresses that your maidens combed, uncared for, all
    hang down ;
The tide has turned, and set the sun that once re-
    splendent shone ;
Thy power—thy wealth and beauty, too—from Babylon
    has gone.

THE BEGGARS.

Who can suppress the endless beggar throng?
Not I, alas ! but here's to them a song ;
They, like the lilies, neither plough nor sow ;
From town to town in happy couples go.

I'll tell you this, they lead a jovial life,
Though hardships in their train be rather rife ;
Duck eggs and ham must grace their boards at tea,
A luxury denied to you and me.

Though oft ill clad, and in a filthy state,
They deem themselves a people wise and great ;
In lodging-houses, hear how they descant
Upon a world in which they seldom want.

Beneath their feet no harvest stubbles bend,
For daily bread on charity depend ;
What do they care how markets rise or fall ;
They've nought to loose by fortune's giddy ball.

None of them labour for a crust of bread;
The world is theirs, and it they lively tread;
No master bids them go do this or that;
Earth's children, they of it the very salt.

No bills to meet upon a certain day,
No fields in crop, no mental trials have they;
Night comes, and with it comes their whole desire,
Their food and bed, what more can they require?

Greedy as the grave, and cunning as the fox
Who steals my chickens and devours my flocks;
Your purse they'd empty; and again refill,
Give them your all, and, lo, they beg you still.

WHEN I WAS YOUNG.

When I was young I strutted with a cane,
Wore handsome gaiters, of my person vain;
My hair I parted like a gentle woman,
And thought myself a bit above the common.

I then was young—about eighteen or so—
My wisdom teeth had not commenced to grow;—
Strok'd my moustache, in colour nearly brown;
My whiskers then were soft as mouse's down.

At tavern bars my evenings spent with nips,
Smoked like a Turk, and laughed between the sips;
Sweet then was life, for me it had no cares,
And, as one blind, I roved 'mid all its snares.

Love-notes, with kisses, came to me per post,
And these my crow quill many a scribble cost ;
Wee, cunning Cupid me a captive led,
And oft my heart has with his arrows bled.

But now, alas ! here with remorse I say,
My spring is past, my summer in decay ;
Seize ye the roses while they blow in June,
Youth's but a blink, and passes thither soon.

THE NOTES O' THE CUCKOO.

The notes o' the cuckoo again usher in
The sweets o' the hawthorn, the blaw o' the whin ;
But what can recall to my bosom again
The form that eternity now must retain ?

The flowerets in blossom bedot the green lea,
But the best, and the dearest, I'll never more see ;
My charmer of life, my helpmate and guide,
Of flowers was the fairest, of women the pride.

But, alas ! cruel death had an eye to her charms,
And bore her away to the tomb in his arms ;
So the cuckoo, the herald of summer, may bring
Glad tidings to others, and birds sweetly sing ;

But to me it can never awake aught but pain,
For it was at this season my charmer was ta'en :
The jewel of life, my compass and crown,
In her heyday of beauty for ever laid down.

And, oh ! thou proud mavis, so high on that tree,
May'st thou never be left with thy nestlings like me ;
Without her I'm lonely, and much her they miss,
For them she had ever a kind word or kiss.

And may I be spared to see them grown up,
Ere I drink the last drop of my strange mingled cup,
For them I shall toil and work with a will,
Till the cold hand of death stops the wheel of life's mill.

Though the notes o' the cuckoo fall soft on the ear,
How I long for a voice that I'll never more hear ;
In my heart there's a void that nothing can fill,
Save the form that lies cold at the foot o' yon hill.

How sacred that spot to this lone heart of mine,
Though it holds but the dust where her spirit did shine ;
I love it, revere it, and never it pass
Without dropping a tear on the green hallowed grass.

But why should I murmur, and thus so complain ?
There's a land—is there not ?—where we'll both meet
    again ;
This, this I will cherish, and long for that sphere
Where far sweeter notes than the cuckoo's I'll hear.

E L L A.

THEN is it so that thou wilt soon
Be wed to one I know not, Ella ?

Where wilt thou spend the honeymoon ?
And hast thou got a good-like fellow ?

You told me once that you would be
An old maid with a cat and parrot ;
I'm glad to hear you've ta'en a man,
And turned your back upon the garret.

A single life, some say 'tis best,
But of old saws I need not blether,
For by this time I know you're fast
Within the noose of wedlock's tether.

And such a tether—Lord, be here,
When thou hast tried years a dizzin ;
Wi' this and that, like a beeskep,
Your head, I trow, will oft be bizzin.

In wedlock there is much to dread,
More than you ever dreamed of, Ella ;
I wish thee well, and I do hope
That you have caught a sober fellow.

BONNIE MARY.

I'LL sing a sang, a wee short sang,
   In praise o' bonnie Mary ;
I thought we couldna hae her lang,
   Sae good a girl was Mary.

Around her bed the angels stood
    In robes that gleam and vary ;
And though they were unseen by us,
    They showed themselves to Mary.

For her pure spirit they had come,
    And it away did carry
To Him who bled upon the cross,
    For He had need o' Mary.

A sweeter rosebud never bloomed ;
    The little guileless fairy
Was loved by a' that e'er her saw,
    So pretty was wee Mary.

A purer blossom couldna be,
    A sweet wee flower was Mary—
Without a spot—and dull our cot,
    Bereft o' bonnie Mary.

She longed to leave this world o' sin,
    And here she grieved to tarry ;
The cup o' death seemed mair than sweet
    To Mary, bonnie Mary.

WEEL DAE I MIND.

Weel dae I mind when first I left
    My mother's clean hearth-stane,
And wander'd forth into the world,
    A sort of second Cain.

What sage advices she me gave,
    And them I threw away ;
But fresh as flowers in vernal June,
    I find them a' the day.

I've seen her pat me on the head,
    And say, " Dae this, ma man ;
Gae to the kirk, yer Bible read,
    And dae the best ye can."

I promised aye to walk up to
    A' rules that she laid doon ;
But scarcely was she oot o' sicht,
    Until I played the loon.

Alas ! my pranks her kind heart griev'd,
    And oft hae I thought shame,
When she discovered a' my tricks,
    To show myself at hame.

Puir bodie, now she's in the grave
    That hallows a' mankind ;
And nought but death can e'er erase
    My mother frae my mind.

Again I feel as when I left
    Her bonnie clean hearth-stane ;
And while I live I'll ne'er forget
    My mother who is gane.

GATHERING FLOWERS.

The cold barren spring brought death to the town—
　Ay, into this fair town of ours ;
He entered the homes of women and men,
　On a mission of gathering flowers.

And he culled the fairest buds on our hearth
　For a brighter and better land ;
And with sorrow we saw them laid in the earth,
　All spoiled by the touch of his hand.

With tears and with sighs we besought him to go,
　And leave the young flowerets alone ;
" Transplanted," he said, " they will much fairer grow,
　And ever bloom fair in that zone,

Where angels and seraphs together abide,
　With Jesus in their peaceful home ;"
And the flowers that we miss are now by His side,
　For the gate to that land is the tomb.

And death is the keeper of that sad gate
　Through which he has gone with our flowers ;
So, with patience and fortitude, teach us to wait
　Till we're gathered like them to his bowers.

WOMAN.

Oh, what had this world been to man
　If woman ne'er had paced it ?

Of bliss poor Adam nothing knew
  Until Eve's lips he tasted.

To man she's said to be a crown,
  And her I much do pride in ;
And were it not but for her smiles,
  This world I could not bide in.

And though that she brought sin and death
  On all, it was for knowledge ;
But 'tis a pity Satan was
  Her tutor when at college.

The cunning serpent her deceived :
  I never see an apple
But what I think on Eden fair,
  And mankind, the first couple.

God pitied Adam all alone
  Within the garden roamin' ;
He saw the use of a helpmate,
  And wisely made a woman.

Oh, what had this world been to man
  If she had ne'er been in it ?
A bleak dull spot, without a flower ;
  But He who did begin it

Gave Adam power o'er fowls and fish,
  And days that none can measure ;
But woman was the rarest gift,
  And best of all his treasure.

AUTHOR OF ALL.

Author of All and everything
　　On earth or in the sea ;
No wonder angels veil their face
　　When gazing upon Thee.

Here as I gaze on the expanse
　　Above, bejewelled bright,
Thy glory I but faintly see,
　　And yet it gems the night.

To me a mystery Thou art,
　　Great Spirit, good and kind ;
Impart to me a clearer light,
　　Illume my darkened mind.

Thy might appears in every form,
　　The winds that round me blow,
Bespeak Thy power, and all the stars
　　Declare it as they glow.

Without beginning, without end,
　　And shall for ever be ;
The hand of time can work no change
　　Upon the brow of Thee.

Thou sittest on the thunder cloud,
　　And walkest on the deep ;
Thy limbs with toil are never tired,
　　Thine eyes require no sleep.

Great Newton, with his giant mind,
   In wonder oft was lost,
Contemplating the bright orbs
   Which Thou hadst hither toss'd

From Thy strong hand athwart the skies,
   Which did the darkness smite,
And filled the world from end to end
   With one grand stream of light.

MARRIED LIFE.

It's saxteen years, I trow, and mair,
   Since you and I were wed ;
And weel, I wot, they've passed away,
   Wi' blythe and lightsome tread.

The wheels o' time gae faster roon'—
   Aye, faster than ye'd think ;
Since you and I were tied, guidwife,
   It hardly seems a blink.

But on together we shall go,
   Wi' hand in hand lock'd fast ;
Through comin' storms we'll maybe get
   As safe as in the past.

What though we're puir as puir can be,
   Sae lang as we hae health,
That's guid enough for you and me,
   We need nae other wealth.

Though whiles we've had enough a-dae
    To get our meat and claes,
We've ne'er been beat, and aye got up
    As yet some tryin' braes.

Twa willin' hearts can overcome
    The steepest brae o' life,
And we ha'e had an unco climb
    Up some o' them, guidwife.

We've reached the summit o' the hill,
    And down the other side
We'll hae to gae wi' shorter steps
    Than in our youthfu' pride.

But never mind, the best maun fail,
    And ye are gey fresh yet ;
Upon the floor, in times gane by,
    None shook a lighter fit.

But we hae danced our fill and mair,
    Our gleesome days are past,
And auld age, wi' his staff in hand,
    Comes stealin' on us fast.

We'll ne'er be young again, guidwife ;
    And when that we are dead,
The grave will be to you and me
    A lasting bridal bed.

WATERING THE DAISIES.

Watering the daisies,
How prettily they smile;
Working in the garden,
Methinks it pleasant toil.

Watering the daisies,
Like soldiers in a row,
All along the border
How beautiful they grow.

Watering the daisies,
And mony other flowers,
No better recreation
For man in leisure hours.

Watering the daisies
That to my mind convey
Better thoughts to guide me,
And cheer me on life's way.

Watering the daisies,
In them I can discern
Lessons more instructive
Than books could e'er me learn.

DEAD ARE THE FLOWERETS.

DEAD are the flowerets that bloomed in the simmer,
    And sae are the roses that blossomed sae braw ;
Thro' clouds grey and gloomy auld Phœbus doth glimmer
    Upon the bleak summit of high Ruberslaw.

How lane-like and dowie the blackbird is sittin'
    Amid the red leaflets on yonder auld tree ;
The winter the lute o' the mavis has smitten,
    And a' the wee birdies are sad as can be.

The landscape around me appears dull and dreary,
    The green hills o' Minto are covered wi' snaw ;
And thro' the bare woodlands winds sigh loud and eerie,
    For the breath o' the winter has ruined ilk shaw.

Cheerless and tame-like the red-breasted robin
    Hops to and fro on the cauld window sill ;
Round my wee cottage the snell breezes sobbin',
    For winter is reigning o'er valley and hill.

Down frae the mountains the fierce floods are sweeping,
    Into the wide bosom of ocean they roll ;
Winter, grim monarch, has all in his keeping,
    And nature seems chilled to the depth of her soul.

Departed has Flora, the pride o' the simmer,
    Her green flowery mantle is blasted and torn ;
Dim o'er the Cheviots auld Phœbus may glimmer,
    But bright he'll ne'er shine till the flowerets return.

THAT DAY I LEFT THE BOWMONTSIDE.

THAT day I left the Bowmontside
  My heart beat sad within me ;
Each ferny glen and rugged peak
  I grieved to leave behind me.

The Slitrig ne'er can glad mine eye ;
  No, it can never charm me ;
Oh for the Bowmont Hills sae high,
  The thoughts o' them still warm me.

I lo'e the bonnie Bowmontside,
  For there I oft did wander
Amongst those hills, with lordly pride,
  Admiring nature's grandeur.

Though stormy clouds the hill-tops hide,
  And dim at times the splendour,
Where will ye find such stalwart men,
  Or maids so fair and tender ?

The Queen of Poesy there resides—
  So sang the bard who found her—
Within a glen, amid the hills,
  With all her maids around her.

And o'er him there she threw a spell,
  With chains mysterious bound him ;
And with a wreath of mountain flowers
  The Queen of Poesy crowned him.

" Go, sing," she said, " of nature's charms,
  Your harp the heart within you ;
On Bowmontside, in future years,
  Capricious fame may find you."

Then from his view that Queen withdrew,
  With all her maids so pretty ;
And, with a heavy heart, him sped
  Unto the restless city,

Where he sojourned, repined, and mourned,
  A stranger to the people ;
And oft he thought of Bowmontside,
  Where plovers weirdly whipple.

The Slitrig cannot glad mine eye ;
  No, it can never charm me ;
Oh for the Bowmont Hills sae high,
  Their rugged wildness warms me.

LINES ON CHARLES HAIG, ATTONBURN,
GONE TO AMERICA.

For Manitoba I am bound,
  By Bowmontside no more I'll roam ;
Adieu, ye weeping ones around,
  For I must leave a much-loved home.

Adieu, adieu, my master kind,
  And a' my friends, so leal and true ;

Another master I may find,
 But find I'll never one like you.

When I am wafted o'er the deep,
 My memory shall back return ;
And I shall often in my sleep
 Revisit lovely Attonburn ;

For there it was I first drew breath,
 And there I've been unto this hour ;
When I forget the Bowmont strath,
 May fate her plagues upon me shower.

My father's hearth I'll ne'er forget,
 Where'er I be I'll to it cling ;
Attest, ye tears that my cheeks wet,
 And all whose hands I warmly wring.

To Thee on high I give the charge
 Of all I love on Bowmontside ;
But on my leaving why enlarge ?
 For cross I must the ocean wide.

So, fare you well, my master true,
 And fare you well, my parents kind ;
My sisters, brothers, all adieu,
 Where'er I roam I shall you mind.

Untrammeled back my heart will come
 Frae yont the sea to Bowmontside ;
In dreams I'll hear the wild bees hum
 On heathy spots, in blooming pride.

And I shall often think upon
   The stream which flows round many a turn ;
And I shall feel right sad and lone,
   When far away from Attonburn.

THE CREATURES OF A DAY.

Oh, what are we ? the creatures of a day,
And, like the flowers, we perish, pass away ;
There's no abiding, no perpetual bliss,
Within a world so full of change as this.

How true, alas ! though we as angels seem,
Our days a shadow, and our nights a dream ;
All have their part, and soon that part is play'd :
We droop and die, and in the grave are laid.

Kings, lords, and princes, men of every state,
Must bow, submissive, to the laws of fate ;
Death comes to all, and none can it evade,
All flesh is grass, and as the flowers we fade.

A few tears shed as we're consigned to earth,
And sorrow soon gives place to bright-eyed mirth ;
Race follows race, and time's impelling wave
Rolls on, and stops but at the silent grave.

From infancy to age we onward creep—
To-day we dance and sing, to-morrow weep ;
From joy to grief, from grief to joy we range ;
Our days and years are few, and full of change.

Alas! we know not what an hour may bring;
Fate twangs his bow, the arrow leaves the string;
Flowers that we love and cherish with delight
Are plucked at noon, and withered ere the night.

Time moves along, the seasons come and go,
Our mirth and mourning have their ebb and flow;
There is no medium in this world of ours,
Where death culls mankind as a child doth flowers.

SIMMER'S AWA'.

THE daisies are fading, and simmer's awa';
Sered are the leaflets, how yellow they fa';
In skies grey and gloomy nae lav'rock I hear,
For simmer's departed, and a' looks sae drear.

I like nae the winter, and view it wi' pain,
And much dae I weary for simmer again;
Nae roses are bloomin' upon the sweet breer
That scented the zephyrs when simmer was here.

The swift-pinioned swallows hae left the auld shed;
The craw-flower and blue-bell sae bonnie are dead;
Nae corncraik at twilight, nae woodlark at morn;
Mute 'mang the red haws the shilfa sits 'lorn.

Nae bairnies are braiding wi' gowans their hair,
For Flora appears in her splendour nae mair;
The ance cheery mavis, a sad bird is he,
Hails nae the birth o' the morning wi' glee.

The blackbird is dowie, a' nature is sad ;
Out on the hillside the herd in his maud
Sees not the bee nor the heather sae braw,
For the sweets o' the simmer are a' gane awa'.

THE REMNANT.

THE remnant of a swarthy race
   Upon the Borders yearn for roamin' ;
How dear to them the camp and chase
   Of hart or hare, at dawn or gloamin'.

Lang syne their sturdy sires would loll,
   For weeks and months, in tents dwelling ;
Made spoons and pans, and trinkets droll,
   While their swart dames went fortune-telling.

These were the days of olden times,
   Of foray raids, blackmail, and juggling ;
Though old, I'll weave them into rhymes,
   And tell you now of whisky smuggling.

In daring bands 'neath Luna's eye,
   Well armed with oaken clubs behind it ;
And long ere Phœbus lit the sky,
   In England sold their stout Glenlivet.

The gaugers rode, and whiles they ran
   Afoot, to catch those lawless fellows,
Who could a raid with Old Nick plan,
   For they were sly and swift as swallows.

Their tall dun chief, or boasted king,
    At fetes athletic had no marrow ;
His praise, O muse, exulting sing,
    And do not chirp it like a sparrow.

A keener sportsman wi' a gun
    Than Wull Faa never went a-shooting ;
He was the very soul o' fun,
    When o'er a dram or at an ooting.

But he has gone from off the scene,
    The days of gipsy glee are over ;
And farmers now nae mair compleen
    Of asses feeding on their clover.

When luckless fate upon them lowered,
    Like leaves by Boreas they were scattered ;
Act after Act them overpowered,
    Till they've been to a remnant tattered.

But it has a' been for their good,
    Against the best we're oft complaining ;
Old customs, barbarous and rude,
    Ill suit an era of new training.

THE GREEN VALE O' BOWMONT.

Oh, Bowmont, thy green vale I love and revere,
Thy people are kind, though at times they are queer ;
Through Scotland I've travelled, but ne'er in my path
Beheld folk sae kind as the folk o' thy strath :

Then hail to the hamlets that nestle beneath
Thy hills on the Border, bedotted wi' heath ;
And hail to the river that rolls through the vale,
Where the fragrance of flowers scents the breeze we
  inhale.

Oh, Bowmont, kind nature upon thee hath smiled,
And has given a charm to thy scenery wild ;
How rapid thy fierce floods : and cold the winds blaw
Round the peaks o' thy mountains covered wi' snaw.

But to see thee adorned in the sweet month o' May,
Our cares we forget and the hairs that are grey ;
How soothing's the scene to a sad wearied breast
To walk in thy glens, on thy mountains to rest.

It calms all our sorrows to see in the morn
The rose o' the briar, the white-blossomed thorn ;
Where'er I may wander thy valley I'll love,
And thy greenwoods, the home of the soft-cooing dove.

TIME.

MEN may decay and perish as a flower,
The cup of life may change from sweet to sour,
But thou, old boy, no change can ever know,
While sun and moon and all the planets glow.

Who can retard thee in thy wayward course?
From whence came thou?—ah! none can tell the source;
Thou wert ere Adam from the earth was made,
Or Lucifer in heaven disobeyed.

When thou began thy reign no man can tell,
Not even the angels cast from heaven to hell;
Before creation who of thee took note?
Beyond all reach art thou of human thought.

On tireless wings thou bear'st thyself away,
And all things perish 'neath thy lordly sway;
Oft do I muse on thee whom none can smite,
And did'st though reign ere this world saw the light

Of that proud sun within the realms of day?
Still on thou marchest, stranger to decay;
Thy strength, old boy, no change can ever know,
While to the moon the oceans ebb and flow.

QUEEN ESTHER.

FROM hamlet to hamlet the sad tidings sped
All over the Border that Esther was dead;
In her "Castle" at Kelso stern death laid her down,
And took from her Highness both sceptre and crown.

And the sceptre she sway'd no more she will sway,
For she's passed from us all to her father, away;
And the fairy-like glamour of Yetholm is gone
With Esther, the last of the strange ancient throne;

For she's laid in the mould, with her forebears at rest—
Of all Gipsy sovereigns we deem'd her the best :
She was honoured by all the great folk of the land,
Who impress'd oft a kiss on her ring-covered hand.

But they'll kiss it no more, and no more she'll be seen
With lords, dukes, and earls upon Kirk Yetholm green;
For the palace is empty, and vacant the throne
Which Esther, the last of the Faas, sat upon, ·

And reigned over a people peculiar, no doubt :
But, of late, they have wandered but little about;
How few, oh, how few in Kirk Yetholm are left,
And the few that are there of their queen have been reft.

They mourn—so they may—for the grand link of old
Has dropped to the bottom of death's dreary hold,
And with it the spell of the Gipsy is broke,
For she was the loadstone and charm of the folk

Who came about Yetholm, in summer so green,
For all had to visit the dainty old Queen ;
To laymen and clergy alike she could speak,
And her bearing at all times was canty and meek.

But with this one or that one she'll ne'er speak again,
From us all, in her " Castle " at Kelso, was ta'en ;
And all loyal subjects without her seem lone,
For with her the glamour of Yetholm is gone.

So tourists may come, and tourists may go,
And the lines o' their loofs to some other show
In that palace up there, to which many have sped
To visit the Queen who is now with the dead.

THE MUMMY KINGS.

Now through the breach of centuries past we look with
    longing eyes,
And, lo, the mighty kings who reigned lang syne the
    world surprise ;
Astonishéd and awe-struck we gaze upon the mummy
    kings,
And wonder at the power which works so many curious
    things.

Who would have thought the searching hand of science
    in her pride
Could ever thus have thrown the veil of countless
    years aside ?
With golden key she has unlocked the secrets of the past,
And light upon the days of old with brilliancy is cast.

Now back to us the Pharaohs come in regal mummy state,
Ye that possess ambitious thoughts here look upon the
    great :
These once were kings—now what are they ?—bereft of
    life and power ;
On bended knees no more the slaves before those
    monarchs cower.

Still with some reverential awe we gaze upon the bones
Of those who once the sceptre swayed, and sat on royal
  thrones ;
Now cleared away the misty doubts anent each pyramid,
The present age with eager hand takes what the ancient
  hid.

Though nought but mummies, still they speak to us of
  other times,
And furnish men with sterling facts above the pitch of
  rhymes ;
From out the mist of perished years they're brought
  before our eyes,
And Egypt well may think those kings of her's a golden
  prize.

When those great kings were in full pomp, none of
  them e'er would dream
That they would through five thousand years of death
  on this age gleam ;
Like beacons they have lighted up the face of all those
  years,
And doubtful history in a dress of purer truth appears.

At last, through science, comes to us the missing links
  of lore,
And God's own book will strengthened be, and treasured
  all the more.
We gather knowledge from the dead : the knowledge
  they impart
Has given to this lettered world another brilliant start.

Now that the tombs have entered been of Egypt's
    mighty kings,
May science soar up higher yet, and broader spread her
    wings ;
Illumined now the Book of Life—a glory on it shed—
And doubting sceptics are convinced by Egypt's mighty
    dead.

Throughout the breach of perished years we gaze, and
    well we may,
Upon those mummies who were kings and tyrants in
    their day,
Upon them look, nor have a wish, for regal pomp and
    power ;
On bended knees no more the slaves need to those
    monarchs cower.

MY PLAID.

My plaid, though faded, auld, and worn,
Wi' a' the fringes frae it torn,
    I lo'e it still ;
Ilk thread o' it my mither spun,
And gave it me, her much-loved son,
    With right goodwill.

Within it rowed when winds were bauld,
It kept me cosy frae the cauld,
    And e'en frae heat :

On simmer days I used to lie
Wi't spread betwixt me and the sky;
    And when 'twas weet .

It screened me frae the draps o' rain
That patt'ring fell upon the plain
    And mountain side.
Beneath it, too, my dog wad cower,
When it came on a heavy shower,
    Wi' collie pride.

And wi' the fairest o' the fair
This well-worn plaid I oft did share
    In youthfu' years.
It's been to me a servant true,
And many a time I it bedew,
    Alas ! with tears.

And for her sake who did prepare
Ilk thread o' it wi' matron care
    I will it wear ;
So long as life pervades my frame,
O' this auld plaid I'll ne'er think shame,
    But it revere.

And when my days on earth are o'er,
Fate grant but this, I'll ask no more,
    When lowly laid
Within my grave, where'er it be,
I charge you all, keep not frae me
    My auld grey plaid.

            G

THE LAMMIES.

The ewes they are bleatin', the lammies are greetin',
    Bereft o' their mithers, they seem a' sae wae ;
To sale-rings they're driven, ties tender are riven,
    That knit them sae closely for many a day.

In the green vale o' Teviot, baith half-bred and Cheviot
    Are downcast and dowie, nae mair dae they play ;
On height and in howie there's many a ewie
    Lamentin' the loss o' their lammies this day.

A' airts they are keekin', their lammies they're seekin',
    But nane 'mang the gowans are sportin' thi' day ;
Changed is the Teviot, and, Borthwick, believe it,
    The ewes ance sae happy are lanely and wae.

Oh, restless they wander amid the wild grandeur,
    Untasted the pasture in glen or on brae ;
Wi' grief they are groanin', and sadly they're moanin',
    The lammies they loved sae are a' ta'en away.

To sale-rings they're driven, ties tender are riven,
    In vale and on mountain what mournin' this day ;
In pens they are bleatin', the bairnies are greetin',
    And echoes that slumbered awake on the brae.

I'm wae for the lammies, bereft o' their mammies,
    The ewes o' the Teviot and Borthwick are wae ;
How sadly they're moanin', how deeply they're groanin',
    The lammies they loved sae are a' ta'en away.

THE WOODS O' THE TEVIOT.

THE woods o' the Teviot are never sae braw
As in the grey autumn, when simmer's awa';
Though nae birds are singin', the lone ear to please,
The glory of autumn encircles the trees.

At sunrise or sunset the fair woodlands gleam
In hues rich and varied, by Teviot's clear stream ;
And dull must the eye be that cannot behold
The woods in their dresses of rich green and gold.

The simmer, though pleasant with birds and with bees,
The autumn outstrips it—how lovely the trees ;
In clusters the red haws the hedgerows adorn,
How gay in their sered robes, though blighted and torn.

A' nature looks pensive, down-hearted, and sad,
Though the woodlands, with beauty, profusely are clad ;
Decay casts a gloom o'er this fair Border land,
And sered are the woodlands, though bonnie and grand.

The greenness o' simmer has left ilka leaf,
For autumn has ta'en it awa' like a thief ;
Though nae birds be singin', and nae flowers in blow,
The woods o' the Teviot exquisitely glow.

THE CAPON TREE.

Thou monarch of the winding Jed,
  By poets named the Capon Tree,
How many years have o'er thee sped?
  Their number I would like to see;
  But now, alas! that ne'er can be,
For they are wafted far away,
And thou art yet in fair array,
And spread'st thy giant arms abroad
Above the green and daisied sod.

Was he a warrior, clad in mail,
  That planted thee by that fair stream;
Thou first of oaks that deck the vale,
  A relic of the past thou seem,
  The shadow of a long-lost dream.
What though a thousand years have fled
Since first thou raised thy crested head,
Thy boughs still o'er the river swing,
And sweet-voiced songsters in them sing.

Thou forest king, so sturdy there,
  Will fleeting time thee ne'er destroy?
Though kindred oak thee upward bear,
  The prop of age thou well employ;
  Birds nest on thee, and lilt with joy,
And 'neath thy branches, far outspread,
The gowans blossom white and red,
And on their petals light the bees,
Which, laden, fly athwart the leas.

Though many twigs forsake thy crest,
    Thy strength has Boreas' might defied;
Beneath thy shade the aged rest,
    And talk of youthful days with pride,
    While past their feet the amber tide
Of Jed goes rippling to the sea;
And lovers meet when day is done,
To breathe their tale where none may see,
Beside the aged Capon Tree.

UNCO MERRY.

I'M aye unco merry when liltin' a sang,
    Amusin' mysel' and a' the wee tots;
Anither ane comes ere the last ane can gang,
    And a' maun ha'e meat for their wee gapin' throats;
Ilk ane I am told's worth a million in gold,
    Their feet o'er the floor beat a right happy measure;
In a house where there's nane, cauld looks the hearth-
        stane,
    Sae what are weans but heavenly treasure?

I'm aye unco merry when liltin' a sang,
    Amusin' mysel': wives whiles are provoking,
Wi' dustin' and washin' they tell us they're thrang,
    And sae at this minute the cradle I'm rockin';
The wee thing looks up in my face, and it smiles,
    Sweet as the rosebud its petals disclosin';
Women and weans, my dear sir, have sic wiles,
    They'd make us believe we're in Eden reposin'.

I'm aye unco merry when liltin' a sang,
　Amusin' mysel' in this autumnal weather.
It's a gey queer house when the wife's out lang,
　Mine's on a visit the now to her mither;
They beat a' for rakin'—they winna bide in—
　Like bees at a skep they cluster and blether;
And here's a wee rogue wi' a scaur on his chin,
　For ilk young imp's past the length o's tether.

I'm aye unco merry when liltin' a sang,
　Amusin' mysel', noo that it's October;
Last night, wi' my lady, I fairly got wrang
　For tastin' a drap, but noo I am sober.
It's strange—is it no?—hoo the siller they'll keep,
　And grudge ane a gless wi' a friend when you're
　　dinin';
And oft wi' their flytin' ane gets little sleep,
　But what is the use o' a body repinin'?

I'm aye unco merry when liltin' a sang,
　The ladies, dear sir, we must not disparage—
My better half's just come in wi' a bang,
　And, losh man, her friends drove hame in a carriage.
And richt prood was I to see her again,
　And soon the bairnies around her were clingin'
As close as ye ever saw fog to a stane,
　While the shouts o' their mirth set the echoes a-
　　ringing.

LAND OF MIST.

Oh, Liddesdale, thou land of mist,
  I lo'e thy benty bogs and rushes,
For there my Nellie first I kissed,
  In yon green haugh where Liddle gushes.

What glowing rapture then I felt, -
  My breast heaved like the great salt ocean;
For there 'twas first my Nellie kent
  The depth of my fond heart's devotion.

I pressed her hand, but couldna speak,
  Wee cunning Cupid's so avenging;
Love makes a body unco weak,
  And hoary time is so estranging.

Ten thousand stars on us look'd down
  That night with their benignant faces,
And, lo, we sat till morning came
  And woke us from our fond embraces.

I'll ne'er forget that balmy night
  We spent amang the scented brackens;
Our covering was the vaulted sky,
  Where the lark soars whene'er it waukens.

Sweet sang the Liddle at our feet,
  I never heard it flow so cheery;
With bliss life's moments seemed complete
  That night by Liddle wi' my dearie.

My rapture was too sweet to last,
    For, don't you know ? the gods had willed
That love's clear sky should be o'ercast,
    And soon the enchanted cup was spilled.

She took the pet—why should I fret ?
    Lang Elliot o' the Haugh had won her ;
Losh, women are a fickle set,
    I'll never court another kimmer.

HERDIN' DAYS.

QUITE true, my freen' ; a' true ye say,
For I ha'e herded in my day
The rakin' kye that aye were fain
To munch at pasture no their ain ;
But, listen an' I'll tell thee noo
Aboot ae auld witch o' a coo

I herded ance.   I mind it weel,
She was a vexin' greedy deil,
That fences brak and ditches lap,
In hedge or dyke aye found a slap,
And after her the rest wad draw,
Her like for thieving nane e'er saw.

To me she was a source o' grief,
And a' folk kent the spotted thief—

Ae horn inturned, the ither oot,
A gutsy, reevin', restless brute,
That never was an hour content—
Frae neeps to corn alternate went ;

At milkin' hours wad tak' the pet,
Then frae her teats nae milk they'd get—
She'd keep it up against their will,
While I was blamed for a' the ill ;
In time o' clegs her tail she'd cock,
And gallop off frae a' the flock.

The glaikit jade, at her I've sworn,
For oot she wadna bide the corn,
Her lang rough tongue roon' it she'd row,
Syne frae the roots it up wad pow ;
Soles o' auld shoon I've seen her eat,
Sae fond was she o' dainty meat.

MY FAVOURITE FLOWERS.

My favourite flowers the snowdrops are,
So humble-like, with drooping head ;
They blossom in the shady wood,
And smile above the sainted dead.

They have a language, and convey
To hearts bereaved a sacred joy,
And tell us of a better life,
A life which death can ne'er destroy.

In churchyards green we like to see
The crocus and the white snowdrop ;
They cast a splendour o'er the scene,
And fill our souls with firmer hope.

As they come forth to greet the spring,
And glad us with their transient bloom,
So we shall rise in radiant robes,
When Christ recalls us from the tomb.

Then sweeter flowers than them we'll see
In bloom ayont the brightest star,
That bathes its brow in yon clear stream ;
My favourite flowers the snowdrops are.

THE BLOW O' THE HAWTHORN.

THE blow o' the hawthorn—I've missed it,
　And missed it right sair has the bee ;
Of a' the sweet blossoms o' simmer,
　The hawthorn is dearest to me.

Our hedgerows and woodlands are pretty,
　But prettier still they had been
If rich-scented blossoms had garnish'd
　The boughs o' the hawthorn sae green.

The zephyrs in morning sae dewy
　Hang wistfully round the haw tree,
And sigh for the sweet fragile blossoms
　That they were accustomed to pree.

Down in the fair valley o' Teviot,
  Where oft on a ramble I go,
I've seen a' the hawthorns quite laden
  With blossoms as white as the snow.

THE MAY-TIME.

THE May-time, it's a cheery time,
  There's aye sae muckle wooin';
And a' the woodlands, far and near,
  Ring wi' the cushie's cooin'.

Kind nature sets the heart alowe,
  For May is aye sae pleasin';
Her balmy breath and scented flowers
  Delights the cuckoo season.

I mind fu' weel, when I was young,
  In May I went a-roamin';
And oft mine ear was ravish'd wi'
  The cuckoo's sang at gloamin'.

The May-time is a merry time,
  It makes a' creatures cheery;
The winter days are well away,
  And nights sae lang and dreary.

Noo at their will the children play,
  And big their wee bit houses;
Now in the burns amang the jukes
  They rear up dams and sluices.

And a' the birds are liltin' crouse,
  For buds baith green and tender
Are opening out their vernal robes
  To wrap the woods in splendour.

Oh, wha could weary when 'tis May?
  There's aye sae muckle sportin'
Wi' lads and lasses out at e'en,
  Beside the hedgerows courtin'.

ALL BARDS ARE POOR.

Few sons of song e'er have a mite to spare,
All bards are poor, and weighted down with care;
Gold is a blessing, if also a curse,
But no true poet ever had a purse.

In London Goldsmith toiled for daily bread,
And slept without a blanket on his bed;
He was so poor that he would grace betimes
A beggar's hovel, though the prince of rhymes.

And Robert Burns, old Scotland's greatest bard,
Despite his genius, lived and died ill-starr'd;
And Greece's minstrel, so historians say,
That Homer begged his bread for many a day.

How strange that great men mostly die quite poor:
Gay won a fortune, lost it in an hour;
Sir Walter Scott with adverse fortune fought,
And never realised the dreams he sought.

Death closed in Greece Lord Byron's brilliant e'e,
And though a lord at home, no peace had he ;
Though fortune deigned on little Pope to fall,
He lived in torment, and tormented all.

Addison in wedlock tried to find relief
From all his cares, but found a sea of grief ;
Capricious fate to bards is oft unkind—
Raleigh was beheaded, Milton he was blind ;

Kirk White in childhood felt the woes of age,
And Chisholm died when nearing manhood's stage ;
Of mighty Shakspeare I have nought to say ;
But come along, thou mellow singer Gray :
Poor Michael Bruce, he sang of genial spring,
And drew his numbers from a tender string.

His lays, though few, in many a book appear ;
And Thomson lives throughout the varied year ;
The Ettrick bard, James Hogg, a happy chiel,
Could sing a sang and tell a story weel.

In Tibbie Shiel's, with other bards he met,
But all are gone, their suns for ever set ;
Now the dark curtain down o'er all I bring :
Most bards are poor, no matter how they sing.

CARLYLE AT THE GRAVE OF HIS WIFE.

OLD as the century, widowed and frail,
  But circled with glory around ;
The great man went like a holy seer,
  And prayed upon sanctified ground,

And there, 'mid the tombs, to God did pray
  By the sacred dust of his wife,
Wearied of fame, and tired of the world,
  For she was the light of his life.

On bended knees he kissed the clay
  Again and again, and he said,
" You were to me the gem of my soul,"
  And tears on her ashes shed.

And, lo, a voice, a musical voice,
  From the spirit-land to him came,
And a flood of joy surg'd through his heart,
  'Twas the voice of his own sweet dame.

And he lingered long on bended knees,
  For spirit to spirit can speak ;
Then wonder not that the warm tears rolled
  Down over his time-withered cheek.

Feeble with age, and nearing the grave,
  How sweet to his ears was that sound ;
And he longed to crumble into dust,
  By the side of her sainted mound.

YOUTH AND TIME.

Iᴛ makes me shudder when I think
    How fast the time gaes on ;
The present year is a' but dune,
    And shortly 'twill be gone.

Ah, treasure time, dear foolish youth,
    For quick it fleets away,
And soon the shades o' gloamin' fa'
    Upon youth's flowery brae.

See'st thou that poor old wearied man,
    Wi' head bowed to his feet,
In his gay manhood never thought
    That time rowed on sae fleet.

Go, ask him now ; he'll shake his head,
    And to you likely say,
" That youth is nothing but a dream,
    And soon the locks turn grey."

Ah ! foolish youth, employ well
    Thy bright and pleasant hours,
For time shall smite thy rosy cheeks,
    As autumn doth the flowers.

Now, back I look to my fair spring,
    And need not tell you why,
That something not unlike a tear
    Comes trickling from mine eye.

Ah ! foolish youth, believe not this,
 That time for thee will stay ;
So waste not thou in pleasure's lap
 Thy little passing day.

THE ZEPHYR.

I'm called a restless zephyr,
 Because I roam at will
Amid the flowers upon the mead
 And on the sunny hill ;
Or down the glens at early dawn,
 Where nature's tears are lying
Like jewels scattered from a crown,
 'Mongst grandeur ever flying.

From place to place I rove about,
 Regardless of repose ;
Now through the woods that grace the dale,
 Or sighing round a rose ;
And for a freak I kiss the cheek
 Of many a pretty maiden,
And from the orchards oft I come
 With sweetest perfume laden.

Scenes ever new I daily view,
 I wander east and west,
I sway the willow by the stream,
 And rock the rooks to rest ;

And for a spree I chase the bee
From gowan unto gowan,
Then o'er the sea I wander free,
Free as the waves there rowin'.

Within the gardens of the great
I wander up and down,
And gather odour for the poor
Within the smoky town ;
I cheer old age with my sweet breath,
I cool the fevered head,
I sprinkle fragrance on the sick,
And bring health to their bed.

Without me dreadful plagues would come
And desolate the land ;
I purify man's vital blood,
And each polluted strand ;
I impart vigour to the weak,
And on my back I bear
Ten thousand blessings to mankind,
Though I be nought but air.

PUIR RAGGED DAVIE.

Puir ragged Davie, there's naebody kens him—
Hoo sune ane's forgotten by when they're puir ;
But ance on a time fu' trig ha'e I seen him,
Spruced up like a gent, wi' a shed in his hair.

H

Towsy and matted his white locks were hanging
    Around his thin haffits, sae bleached-like and pale ;
For a crust, on the street a song he was singing,
    His last copper spent on a tumbler o' ale.

Yet oft ha'e I seen him wi' pouchfu's o' siller,
    And crouse as a lammie that skips o'er the swaird ;
He drank wi' the smith, and he tea'd wi' the miller,
    For few wi' puir Davie could then be compared.

His auld decent mither, she left him a posy
    That micht weel ha'e saired him the hail o' his days ;
He was then weel to dae, being young, fresh, and rosy ;
    But noo he's a shadow in auld greasy claes.

In vile dirty hovels he lies down at e'ening,
    Contented and happy as mortal can be ;
When sunk in the mire, what's the use o' compleenin' ?
    And with me, my readers, I think you'll agree.

I stood when I heard him upon the street singing,
    His voice, weak and broken, fell sad on my ear,
And few to puir Davie a copper were flinging,
    And yet o'er his face strayed a gleam of good cheer.

But come awa', Davie, I'll never despise ye,
    You owned me when wealthy, I'll own thee when
        puir ;
An old pair o' trousers and sark I shall gi'e thee,
    And a' the few shillings that I ha'e to spare.

MERRY JOCK.

MERRY JOCK o' Bowmontside,
 Happy Jock o' Bowmontside,
Has got a wifie o' his ain,
 Alane the bodie couldna bide.

Nae mair the rover gangs frae hame ;
 Merry Jock o' Bowmontside
Sits cantie by his ingle flame,
 The brichtest on the Bowmontside.

Now little urchins round him craw,
 Merry Jock o' Bowmontside
The cradle rocks at gloamin' fa',
 Fu' happy at his ain fireside.

To Bacchus' shrine nae mair gaes he ;
 Merry Jock, the prince o' men,
Has twined the thread as it should be,
 And keeps at e'en his ain fire-en'.

The web of peace now fills the loom ;
 Merry Jock o' Bowmontside
Has got a lassie in her bloom ;
 Alane the bodie couldna bide.

HELEN'S LAMENT.

At Fasten's E'en, when ba's are played,
　I'll look for ane that is nae here;
Wi' downcast heart I'll watch their mirth,
　And wipe away the briny tear.

They tell me that I shouldna mourn—
　'Tis easy for them sae to speak;
Amongst the crowds that shout and laugh,
　For my ain love I needna seek.

Grief, like the sea, may ebb and flow,
　And joy for ever may subside;
'Tis sae wi' me, for sorrow's wave
　Rolls through my heart at highest tide.

Though sad our lot, we must submit,
　There's hearts of others reft and torn;
The cruel fates that frown to-day,
　Wha kens but they may smile the morn?

Yes, smile they may, but not on me,
　The die for life it has been cast,
And sorrow's wail rings o'er the vale
　Where holy hands made our hearts fast.

Alas! those hills nae mair I'll climb,
　Nor tread the glens where brackens grow;
I'll wrap me in my wandering cloak,
　And say farewell to Bowmont now.

JESSIE.

THOU art, indeed, the fairest flower
　In garden grove, on mead or lea;
But fate me calls, and I must go
　Away, my Jessie, far from thee.

By all the powers, this vow I make,
　So deign to listen, Jessie, love;
No other maid I'll ever wed,
　If thou but to me constant prove.

I'll soon be on the restless deep,
　And sailing, swan-like, o'er the blue
Expanse of waters far away—
　Away from Teviotdale and you.

Then fare you well, my Jessie dear,
　And should we never meet again,
No other maid shall ever have
　The heart to which I now thee strain.

A few hours more, and I must step
　Upon that ship about to sail;
And none I grieve to leave but you,
　The fairest flower o' Teviotdale.

THE FROG.

Oh, spare the wanderer in thy way,
　Why live with all at strife?
From fly or worm I would not take
　The little spark of life.

For I this life of mine enjoy,
  And they must e'en love theirs ;
But ruthless man a tyrant is,
  And spare, he never spares.

Be't his own kind or other race,
  Blood, blood, the wretch must spill ;
Like vulture ever in his heart,
  The ardent wish to kill.

Why such a wish should ever reign
  Within the human breast
I cannot tell, though Cain at first
  By shedding blood transgressed.

And since that time, who can recount
  The actions men have done ?
For cruelty we far surpass
  All creatures 'neath the sun.

THE THRUSH.

Sing on, sing on, how sweet thy strain,
It rings athwart the daisied plain,
  And elevates my heart ;
Sing on, sweet bird, and sing to me,
For well I love thy notes of glee,
  Which thou to all impart.

Oh, what a rapture in thy lay,
It draws my soul from Satan's sway,
  And brings me nearer God ;

Within the town, where riot drains
The vital tides of young warm veins,
  And deathward paves the road ;

Thou singest not in lane or street,
Nought but the tramp of busy feet
  Within the mart of toil ;
But here, within the bushy glen,
Not ruined yet by thoughtless men,
  I see fair nature smile.

Sing on, sing on, that song of thine
Brings joy to this heart of mine,
  Thou bird without a peer ;
Sing on harmoniously the chime
Of all thy notes, and could I rhyme
  Such notes as those I hear,

I would feel proud as proud could be ;
But whistle on, and sing to me
  A ditty sweet and rare ;
Without you what would be the vale ?
A dowie scene where I would wail,
  And languish in despair.

Sing on, sing on, thou mellow thrush,
Sweet minstrel, on that hawthorn bush,
  No bard can rival thee ;
Thou art, indeed, the king of song,
And curst be those that would you wrong,
  By heaven and by me.

SPRING.

Now winter is over,
   And Sol's kindly heat
Causeth the pulses
   Of nature to beat.

The song o' the mavis,
   So mellow and clear,
Adown in yon thicket
   At morning I hear.

There's mirth in the woodland,
   There's mirth on the lea,
For spring is the season
   Of wooing and glee.

Like a bride at the altar,
   So gaily she's dressed,
With flowers round her head,
   And a rose in her breast.

The winter's departed,
   Of her he's afraid ;
With feet deckt with daisies,
   She walks through the glade.

On her brow there is sunshine,
   The brightest, I ween,
And her garments surpasseth
   The robes of a queen.

She skips o'er the mountains,
   She laughs in the vale,
And song-birds with ditties
   The sweetest her hail.

SUMMER.

O WELCOME, fair summer,
   Trip over the plain,
For thee, deckt with blossom,
   Thrice welcome again.

With thee, fairy summer,
   There's none to compare,
For roses and pansies
   Are wove in thy hair.

Oh, welcome, fair summer,
   The bright stars and moon
Look down on thy beauty
   In beautiful June.

I ne'er saw a maiden
   So lovely and gay,
For the sheen of thy splendour
   Bedazzles the day.

O'er thy brow the laburnum's
   Rare tassels hang down;
And the blow o' the hawthorn
   Adorneth thy gown.

Oh, welcome, fair summer,
And stay with us long,
Thou queen of the seasons
And theme of my song.

AURORA BOREALIS.

AURORA BOREALIS !
With wonder you fill us ;
Clothed in a splendour
Which dazzles the eye ;
Making the zenith bright,
Flashing through dreary night,
And spreading a glory
All over the sky.

Aurora borealis !
With wonder you fill, us ;
Seldom, if ever,
Such grandeur was seen ;
Rare child of beauty, you,
Robed in the rainbow's hue,
Lighting up ether
With thy gorgeous sheen.

DENHOLM DEAN.

FAIR Denholm Dean, thy praises have been sung
By many a bard whose harp is now unstrung ;
Here, underneath the shade of birchen boughs,
I court the muse, and hurriedly compose.

My verses, all undressed, with rapture sing,
Where Leyden spent fair childhood's pleasant spring ;
Home of the mavis, piping loud and clear,
From Boreas guarded by that frowning seer,

Dark Ruberslaw, with cloud-encircled head,
No more shall Leyden thy proud summit tread ;
In far-off India, laid him down to rest,
With heart and soul which loved thy craggy breast.

In thee, fair dean, the poet often tród,
Admiring thee and all the works of God ;
Of lordly Minto's woods and rocks he sung
With all the languages upon his tongue.

Home of the bard that perished far from here,
Enshrined in song by one without a peer ;
His fiery genius oft didst thou evoke,
His " Scenes of Infancy " a master stroke.

NEW YEAR'S DAY.

FIE, haste ye, dame, it's twelve o'clock,
   Our neighbours a', they'll sune be here,
Sae ye maun bring the dainties ben,
   And no be shabby this New Year.

Gae snod the bairns, and smooth yere locks,
   Noo, like my ain, turned thin and grey ;
It's hard to tell wha may come in,
   Sae dress fu' neat this New Year's Day.

Hark ! hear the bells of tower and town
    Send forth their greetings to the morn ;
The infant year, pure frae God's hand,
    Has been, 'mid shouts of rapture, born.

Lo, the first-fitters, here they come ;
    Fie, haste ye, dame, throw wide the door,
They gather round grandfather's bed,
    Who minds the cares of age no more.

With palsied hand he takes the glass,
    And wishes a' a happy year ;
Blood-stirring airs make moments pass
    On golden wings that bring us cheer.

Like roes upon the mountain side,
    The youngsters lightly dance and fling ;
For a' the goodwife spreads the board,
    Proud of her goose, wi' neck 'neath wing.

The fiddle stops.   Quoth the crouse dame,
    " Sit forward : pree the good things here ;"
A roasted pig the table graced,
    Within its mouth a jolly pear.

Her dainties, they were praised by a',
    But most was said about the cakes ;
She smiled, well pleased, and, bashful, said,
    " I baked them specially for your sakes ;

For John and me have lost our teeth,
  Of oaten cakes we nought can mak' ;"
Her goose and pig wore out o' sight ˙
  Despite the entertainin' crack.

All satisfied, they seek the floor,
  The friendly glass goes round again ;
Ho, fiddler, touch thy strings of glee,
  For nimble feet await the strain,

Elate with pleasure, one and all,
  Commingle in the blythesome reel ;
Life's changeful cup ne'er held such sweets,
  And they the sweets o't seemed to feel.

With mirth the year has been begun,
  Ne'er mind the old, 'tis past and gane ;
Let's hope there is for a' mankind
  A blessing in the new one's reign.

ST. KILDA.

St. Kilda, thou pride of the Highlands,
  Begirt by the wide-rolling sea ;
There's none of the western islands
  So stern-like and rugged as thee.

Thou dark misty isle, which the ocean
  In sunshine or storm ever laves ;
Above you the sea gulls in motion,
  Around you the snake-crested waves.

Yes, thou art the home of the true Gael,
　　Unconquered by Roman or Dane ;
Around you the breakers meet, sigh, and wail,
　　And beateth thy stout rocks in vain.

Oh, had I the power of description,
　　I'd draw such a picture of thee,
I'd make you without all deception
　　The stout island king of the sea.

St. Kilda, surrounded by waters
　　That rush round the rim of the world ;
Thine are the beautiful daughters,
　　With dark eyes and raven locks curled.

Thy sons are the princes of manhood,
　　And strong as the rocks that they climb
In quest of the great fulmar's young brood
　　That nestle on crags steep and grim.

St. Kilda, thou gem of the Highlands,
　　Or Patmos encircled by sea ;
There's none of the western islands
　　So stern-like and rugged as thee.

TEVIOTDALE.

Fair Teviotdale, thou art the land
　　Of Scott and Leyden's lore ;
Thy mountain streams have oft been tinged
　　With blood in days of yore ;

But now industry spreads her wings
   O'er thee, the very chart .
Of peace and commerce, and thy sons
   Have made thee labour's mart.

No more thy hills with beacons blaze,
   Fair Teviot, richly crowned,
With warlike poesy and the harp
   Of Scott shall ever sound ;
Thy reivers he from darkness snatch'd,
   And placed them in the light,
With fancy rare has clothed them all
   In robes that nought can blight.

Thy ancient chiefs at his command,
   Upon the Borders wide,
Came from the depth of byegone time
   In all their doughty pride.
The veil he lifted off the past,
   And had it not been him,
Our Border land, so fraught with mist,
   Had been a shader dim.

Thy old grey towers point to the days
   When warriors, clad in mail,
Hanged Englishmen, who were their foes,
   On trees that deck the dale ;
At Branxholm yet there is a tree
   On which those foemen hung,
And old tradition 's given it
   A warlike-speaking tongue.

From dark obscurity he raised
　　Thy mighty men of old ;
And foray raids, in martial strains,
　　By him are nobly told ;
To future ages conjured up
　　The legends of the past,
A halo o'er them he has flung
　　Which shall for ever last.

THE VOICE OF GOD.

THE voice of God rings in my ears
　　Whenever I do wrong ;
My faith is weak, but I will pray
　　To Him who'll make it strong ;
Temptations come with faces fair,
　　And they me oft deceive,
And, to my cost, I often find,
　　Like David, cause to grieve.

Without His aid, what would I be ?
　　A leaf toss'd by the wind ;
Ay, worse than that—an abject worm,
　　And, like it, just as blind ;
But He is good, and full of love,
　　And though He may us try,
We should resist besetting sins,
　　And pass them coldly by.

Who have not felt their hearts at times
  Throb between good and ill ?
The balance beam is sure to hang
  Just as the scales we fill.
My passions, headlong as a stream
  Which in full flood doth roll,
I try to curb as well 's I can,
  But cannot them control.

Therefore to God I'll upward look,
  And unto Him I'll pray
To give me strength to cope with all
  Temptations in my way ;
For many rise up in my path,
  And, oh, they seem too fair ;
It's hard, indeed, to think that they
  Would ever me ensnare.

LIFE.

Oh, what's the world ? 'Tis nought to me,
  For I must go and leave it ; .
My life's a stream, and flowing free,
  Though I may not perceive it.

A few years more—perhaps an hour ;
  Nay, less—perhaps a minute—
Till I am blasted like a flower,
  Uncertainty is in it.

My life is but a slender thread,
   And careless oft I spin it ;
By passion's wildest fancy led,
   This way and that I win it.

In youth I thought life had no cares,
   But cares I find are in it,
On every side alluring snares
   To tempt me as I spin it.

My spring is past, my summer's come,
   Wi' disappointments in it ;
But on life's ills I'll set my thumb,
   And whistle like a linnet.

My vigorous prime, 'twill soon glide by—
   Old age, with fear I view it ;
'Tis not that I'm afraid to die,
   But how I may get through it.

To be a burden on my friends,
   Or in a poorhouse plantit ;
Such thoughts as these my bosom rends,
   And make me oft look dauntit.

No miser's wish for gold have I,
   And little do I heed it ;
Yet a few pounds put careful by
   For old age may be needit.

Then let me strive yet to obtain
    This wish, if fortune will it :
That I at last my grave may gain,
    On independence billowit.

WHAT IS LIFE?

OH, what is life? has oft been asked,
    The while we sojourn here ;
Ye'll see a smile on this one's lip,
    On that one's cheek a tear.

We are but tenants here at will,
    And maybe at our birth
'Twas written down how many years
    We had to spend on earth.

But be they many, or be they few,
    I'll ever be content,
Since life is but a vital spark,
    To us a season lent.

I'll thankfu' be, howe'er I fare
    Upon life's ocean wide ;
Wi' grief I see my fellow men
    Sink down on every side.

And wi' those mariners o' the past
    Some day I shall be laid,
And covered up wi' little pomp,
    When once my part is played.

THE HAWTHORN O' THE GLEN.

Away, far up amid the hills,
　Far from the homes o' men,
There is a tree, a bonnie tree,
　A' blossom in the glen ;

And by whose hand 'twas planted there,
　It puzzles me to know :
Perhaps the winds, the stormy winds,
　They there a seed did blow.

'Tis said that flowers in deserts bloom,
　And perish oft unseen ;
'Tis sweeter scented than the broom,
　And long discovered been.

And though 'tis not on pampered soil,
　It scents as sweet the air
As any that I ever saw
　Reared up wi' greater care.

How long it has adorned the wilds
　No one can me inform ;
It shields the shepherd from the heat,
　And screens him from the storm.

Long may it ornament the glen,
　And time it ne'er deface ;
Around its gnarled and sturdy trunk
　The lambs have many a race.

Without it what would be the glen ?
A barren spot, indeed ;
But God is wise, and bade the winds
Waft there a hawthorn seed.

THE MOUNTAIN STREAM.

LEAPING, laughing—lo, it comes
From yonder sunny hill ;
Clear as crystal, on it rolls
With blythe and happy trill.

Along its daisied, grassy banks
The harmless lambkins play ;
And in the leafy birchen bowers
The songsters sing all day.

Full of health the amber tide,
Befringed with willows grand,
Rolls onward for the good of all,
A blessing from God's hand.

Ye that dwell in smoky towns,
But come and see the rill
Which turns for sport the giant wheel
Of yonder grinding mill.

'Tis full of prattle as a child
Upon its mother's knee ;
What need I care for rivers grand ?
A mountain stream for me.

SECOND LOVE.

In love again—a pleasant state ;
But were you not in tears of late,
  For one that's gone ?
Oh ! can it be, the callous heart
So soon forgets those that depart,
  And leave it lone ?
With Mary now on kisses fed,
Ah, me ! the best are soon forgot,
  When they are dead.

Dost ne'er look back unto the hours
You roved with Kate amid the flowers—
Her shade doth William never see
  With moistened eye.
Oh ! can it be that she's forgot,
Who once engrossed thy every thought
  By night and day ?
Too soon, alas ! are all forgot
  When passed away.

LIZZIE.

Out in the garden, with roses
In blossom around her doth sit,
The fair, matchless maiden o' Teviot,
Sweet Lizzie, the pride o' Woodfit.

There, in the garden, 'mid roses,
Ye'll see her at sweet gloamin' fa'
Tending the daisies and pansies,
Her ainsel' the fairest o' a'.

High on the green boughs above her,
The song-birds they cheerily twit;
And a' the braw lads o' the Borthwick
Are sighin' for Liz o' Woodfit.

Spotless and pure as the blossom
Of yonder gay blooming haw-tree;
And a modester maiden than Lizzie
Nae mortal on Teviot could see.

There, in the garden, 'mid roses,
The fair queen of beauty doth sit,
Plying her needle, unconscious
That she is the pride o' Woodfit.

BOWMONTSIDE.

Oh, Bowmontside, thou fairy spot,
  For thee my bosom yet doth burn;
In foreign land, where I now stand,
  To thee mine eyes I often turn.

Can I forget the murmuring streams
  That wind so clear on Bowmontside?
Oh, no, I see them in my dreams,
  My dreams ayont the foaming tide.

E'en where I stand, methinks I hear
  The music o' the Bowmont rills;
And oft I climb with childish glee
  When dreaming thus my native hills.

What though I rove 'mid fairest scenes ?
   Their lavish splendour cannot please
An exile bound with fairy chains,
   Far from his home ayont the seas.

Oh, land of dark-eyed angel nymphs,
   My very soul seems part of you ;
And oft I gaze, through miles of haze,
   Across the ocean deep and blue.

Fain would I tread again the hills,
   The verdant hills o' Bowmontside ;
In vain the wish, for I must stay
   Ayont the ocean salt and wide.

MY NATIVE LAND.

THAT day I left my native land
   My heart was sad, I scarce could speak ;
My father sighed, and pressed my hand—
   My mother wept, and kiss'd my cheek.

My brothers and my sisters, too,
   All bathed in tears, around me clung ;
And when I said to them, " Adieu !"
   Grief almost overpowered my tongue.

Then, " Fare you well," my mother said,
   And clasp'd me to her care-worn breast ;
" I'll take a lock from off the head
   Which never here again may rest."

" Yes, take a lock, my mother dear,
   And give me one of yours, though grey,
With father's twined, I will them wear
   Upon my heart, when far away :

When far away from Bowmontside,
   Far out upon the restless sea,
Within a world of waters wide,
   These locks my comforters shall be.

And if I ever reach that shore,
   That far-off place to which I sail,
I'll miss the whins and hawthorn hoar
   Which maketh fair my native vale.

My native land, adieu, adieu !
   Ye scenes of childhood, wild and grand,
Where I the breath of life first drew,
   And mother led me by the hand.

Those days are sped, and I must go
   To other lands ayont the deep ;
O God, around my parents throw
   Thy mighty arms, and safe them keep.

My father's hearth I'll ne'er forget,
   No matter where fate makes me roam ;
Like jewels in rich trappings set,
   My heart remains at home, sweet home.

THE ANGEL OF DEATH.

Out of the east came the angel of death,
   With his pinions outspread to the wind ;
And he smote in our vale with his chilly breath
   All the sweet little buds he could find.

To shield them from him we tried all we could,
   ·But our efforts and tears were in vain,
For over them all that angel did brood,
   Leaving sorrow and woe in his train.

And with bruised, bleeding hearts we gathered the buds,
   Bereft of their beauty and bloom ;
And under the shadow of dark low'ring clouds
   We bore them away to the tomb.

There we covered them up, in the lone churchyard,
   To their Father in heaven restored ;
And we left them asleep, 'neath the vernal sward,
   For death was sent out by the Lord

To fetch Him the buds that we laid in the grave ;
   And though that their want leaves a blank,
We know He's but taken the blooms that He gave,
   So at all times the Lord let us thank.

HERMITAGE.

BENEATH the mottled autumn sky,
  With comrades twa in Herm'age dale,
On the brown sward we down did lie,
  And spake of many a warlike tale.

With pride we viewed the castle o'er,
  And thought of byegone warriors brave
Who strod in armour here before
  Those walls which guard the giant's grave.

If all be true which records tell,
  The " Cout " of Keilder here is laid ;
In that deep pool, 'tis said, he fell,
  And it we wond'ringly surveyed.

Oh, ancient castle, grim and grey,
  Where are thy feudal chieftains now ?
Thou relic of a former day,
  With centuries upon thy brow,

Speak out, and tell us where are they
  Who trampled under foot the law,
And o'er the Border hills held sway,
  Where they langsyne did kings o'er-awe.

Within thy lonely courts no more
  Resound the tramp of arméd men,
A stillness reigns o'er all the shore,
  And peace presides in every glen.

THE WINTER TIME.

There's a beauty in the autumn,
    When the leaves are red and sere ;
But there is a fairy splendour
    When the winter time is here.

There's a beauty in the streamlets
    When ice-bound from side to side,
And the youth of town and country
    Skating on them in full pride.

There's a beauty in the winter,
    And a vigorating power ;
And though no birds be singing
    At the bonnie gloamin' hour,

There's a pleasure, pure and holy,
    Broodin' o'er the cottar's hearth,
Where a group of happy faces
    Make his heaven upon earth.

There's a beauty in the winter,
    And though he's fierce and stern,
He has beauties, many beauties,
    If we could them but discern.

THE MAID O' WOODFIT.

Of Border maidens she's the flower,
  Whose like on Borthwick none e'er saw—
Within her eyes a witching power
  That might the angels downward draw.

Though I ha'e roamed on Borthwick braes,
  And wandered through the shady woods
Where song-birds sing their sweetest lays,
  And cushats tend their downy broods,

I never spied a fairer maid :
  Her form is matchless and her mien ;
The lily in the greenwood shade
  Can look no modester, I ween.

On Borthwick braes the flowers may blaw,
  And feast wi' sweets the eident bee,
And dewdrops on their bosoms fa'
  When gloamin' steals athwart the lea ;

But wi' my charmer none can vie,
  Her Grecian brow and breast of snow,
Whereon the pure white roses lie,
  In fullest beauty all aglow.

She's fairer far than any flower
  That ever graced the Borthwick stream ;
Nae rosebud wet wi' genial shower
  Could fresher look or purer seem.

MAY WITH THE HAZEL EYES.

MAY with the hazel eyes,
  Glances that move me,
Bright as that lonely star
  Shining above me.

Lips ripe and ruddy,
  The reddest e'er seen ;
Two rows of snowy teeth
  Glistening between.

Over a white brow
  The wavy curls hinging,
Backwards and forwards
  The zephyrs them flinging.

May with the hazel eyes,
  Lightsome and fleet,
How queenly and stately,
  A goddess complete.   .

Foot there was never
  A neater set down ;
Flower of perfection,
  And pride of the town.

Her waist the frail lily stem
  In the wood shade ;
Her bosom the white rose,
  The first of the glade.

Maid there was never
    A lovelier one ;
The face of this fairy
    The bright morning sun.

AMONG THE BIRKS.

AMONG the birks o' bonnie Wells
    I looked, and, lo, there saw
The ornamental trees of old
    Before the woodmen fa'.

I listened to the powerful axe,
    Which thrilled my very frame ;
And to the earth, with doleful sound,
    The trees of beauty came.

O'ercome with grief to see them fall,
    I begged of them to spare
The giant trees which long had made
    The landscape look so fair.

On me they gazed with eyes of scorn,
    " Know'st thou not this ?" they said,
" Who can recall the fatal shaft
    Which from the bow has sped ?"

" Oh, spare those old baronial trees,"
    I cried again, aloud ;
"The birds them loved, and many an eye
    Of them was more than proud."

But would they stop?—no, on they went,
    Determined to deface
The monarchs that had beautified
    For centuries the place.

For ages yet they might have stood
    With vigour in their arms;
But oh, alas! they're hewn down,
    And robb'd of all their charms.

On withered heaps of mangled boughs,
    The songsters chirp, depress'd,
For scarce a tree for them now stands
    Whereon to build a nest.

In flocks the doves confounded fly
    Unto the shrubless wild;
For ruin stern holds regal sway
    Where once kind nature smiled.

O Wells, fair Wells, for thee I mourn;
    No more the summer breeze
Shall linger, as in days of old,
    Amongst thy stately trees;

For they are levelled with the ground:
    The ground whereon they grew
Reminds me of some battle field
    Where death his thousands slew.

Though here and there some veterans stand,
   Of all their kin bereft ;
They, too, shall fall, and that ere long,
   Though for a season left.

Old oaks, the pride of many a laird
   Who lived at bonnie Wells,
I charge you now to look about
   The safety of yourselves.

The garden quite neglected is,
   No one for it to care ;
And gravel walks, with fog o'ergrown,
   Call loudly for repair.

Adieu, fair Wells, I gladly quit
   Thy mutilated glade,
For who can look without regret
   Upon thy ruined shade ?

Years, countless years, may come and go,
   And heirs thee still retain ;
But what thou wert in former years
   Thou'lt never be again.

LIFE.

LIFE has been likened to a stream
   With many a turn ;
In youth a river wide and deep,
   In age a burn.

K

Within its short and clouded span
　　Both sweets and gall ;
And tireless time, with mighty broom,
　　Graveward sweeps all.

To flowers mankind have likened been
　　By many a wit,
Who have in verse and sober prose
　　Of mankind writ.

Like them we're culled in every stage
　　By death's cold hand,
And borne like bubbles on the main
　　To that strange land

Where all doth from their labours rest
　　In calm repose ;
Life has been likened to a stream,
　　Yet deathward flows.

Into eternity it runs,
　　And there doth end
That little span of fleeting life,
　　Not ill to spend.

THE WHITE KING.

Ah, me ! ah, me ! the white king comes,
　　And yellow leaves are fa'in' ;
'Twill sune be winter, and the snaw
　　In wreathes together blawin'.

The bonnie flowerets fade awa'
  Wi' sorrow on their faces,
For autumn in his robes o' grey
  The sweets o' simmer chases.

Fu' silent sits the blackbird noo,
  The sered leaves roond it lyin',
For autumn treads the woodlands through,
  Where Boreas' self is sighin'.

Ah, me! ah, me! the simmer's gane,
  The white king back returning;
His chilly breath and chilly rain
  Sets nature a' a-mourning.

Nae swallows near the auld cot flee,
  They kent the king was comin';
And sae they've gane ayont the sea,
  Where instinct did them summon.

And after them I fain would gae,
  For winter's cauld and hoary;
Though skaters skate, and curlers play,
  And in the white king glory.

IRELAND.

POUR out to that distracted land
  A flowing cup;
May landlords and their tenants soon
  Together sup.

Stamp out the evils that exist
  In the green isle ;
O Lord of Hosts, remember it,
  Upon it smile.

Bless thou the land wherein
  The shamrock grows,
And teach mankind to be
  No longer foes.

Raise up the weak, down-trodden,
  And depress'd ;
By murder wrongs can never
  Be redress'd.

Enough of blood for nothing
  Has been shed ;
The robe of peace, O Lord,
  O'er Ireland spread :

That glorious land, the birthplace
  Of the brave
And Thomas Moore : from ruin,
  Lord, it save.

SLITRIG BELLA.

I've sung o' Borthwick's fairy maids,
  And Teviot's too ; but this I tell ye,
There's no a fairer in the land
  Than bonnie, bloomin' Slitrig Bella.

Of ideal maids I'm sick and tired,
 For one that's real I've long been itching ;
And by the sacred Nine, I swear,
 That she's a beauty quite bewitching.

And though she's but a lassie yet,
 With child-like notions to her clinging,
No flower in blow could fairer be,
 And none so worthy of my singing.

In a few years, if she be spared,
 She'll take the eye of many a fellow ;
And, by the bye, he may feel proud
 Who wons the heart of bonnie Bella.

She's fair as any new-blown rose
 With dew upon its bosom lying ;
And o'er her lofty, snowy brow
 The glossy auburn ringlets flying.

Though novels I have oft perused,
 And read therein of charming creatures,
In fiction's field I never found
 A maid with such angelic features.

Of matchless maids I've seen not few :
 And this with pride again I tell ye,
There's not a fairer in the land
 Than bonnie, blooming Slitrig Bella.

SHE PRAYS FOR ME.

She prays for me, the little dear,
   I know it to be true ;
What wonder, then, if burning tears
   My careworn cheeks bedew.

Lost in a labyrinth of vile sin,
   .She found me sunk in night ;
And led me to a purer path,
   A path of glorious light.

" Walk there," the godly maiden said,
   And, pointing to the skies,
" My Father there inviteth thee,
   No sinner He denies.

" Why did'st thou walk in such a path ?
   Know this," the maid did say,
" There's but one road to heaven leads,
   All others lead astray."

AN HONEST DOG.

An honest dog was Clyde, and true,
In fun against me he wad pu',
At string he'd tug or leather strap ;
For want of these I've used my cap,
And when he got it oot my han',
Wi' it how proud and pleased he ran.

Then him I'd chase to get it back,
Lest he it a' in holes wad chack ;
Owre knowes, through howes, wi' it he'd rin,
Then pause till I was just within
A good Scotch pace of him or so,
Give one loud bark, when off he'd go.

Thus hours we spent fu' sweet thegither,
Though but a dog, I ca'd him brither ;
Unlike mankind, could not deceive,
He was an honest dog, believe ;
Frae him ilk mornin', when we met,
A hearty welcome I wad get.

He'd whine and bark, upon me loup,
And in his nonsense whiles he'd coup
The toddlin' bairns aboot the place,
And after that wad lick their face ;
Wad roon' them rin, and wi' his daffin'
Sune pleased them a', and had them laughin'.

But past those days, and he is dead,
The wisest collie ever bred ;
My steps he watched in early years,
And off my cheeks has licked the tears ;
Above him noo the sods are green,
And boyish tears come to my een.

JOANNA.

Tell Joanna, my dear sister,
    That I love her winning way;
To me she seems as guileless
    As yon lammie on the brae.

No, I never saw another
    Sae endowed wi' sense and grace;
Sweet innocence is stamped upon
    Her bright and sunny face.

And o'er her cheeks may sorrow's tears
    Never have cause to roll;
To see her grieved 'twould break my heart,
    And wreck my peace of soul.

MET HER BY CHANCE.

I met her by chance one starry night
    Walking alone, outside of the town;
In her bonnet a rose of the purest white,
    While over her brow hung the ringlets brown.

"Good evening," I said, and she gaily smiled,
    And her small soft hand in my own I took;
Then, arm in arm, away we whiled
    Old father Time in a quiet nook.

We spoke of the delicate topic of love,
The fount and the cause of a thousand sighs;
And her gentle voice was like that of a dove
In the depth of a wood at sweet sunrise.

So enrapt were we that old father Time,
Unheeded, unnoted, the swift hours stole;
For lovers live in a fairy clime
When under the sway of Cupid's control.

From lips, which a sculptor a model might make,
Of burning kisses I had not a few;
But the song of the thrush at dawn in the break
Compelled us to sunder, and sigh an adieu.

THE LAST DAY O' THE YEAR.

This is the last day o' the year,
It dies, and with a snowy head;
And when for ever it has fled
We'll drink and dance above its bier.

How strange that we should glory in
The steady march of endless time;
A subject fit for any rhyme,
And so with pride I'll now begin

My song, a requiem for the year;
To others I shall leave the new,
Because the auld I ha'e got through,
With many a hope and many a fear.

We know what has been in the auld,
But of the new we cannot speak ;
Yet when it comes we'll kiss its cheek,
And it we'll to our bosom fauld.

At twenty-one we all things know,
At thirty wauken from a dream,
At forty we sail down the stream,
And, like the passing year, must go.

The promised age, threescore and ten,
What is it but one changeful hour?
But change has such a pleasing power
That it ne'er fails in pleasing men.

But to my theme I'll now return,
From it I've wandered rather far,
For evening comes with many a star
To light the old year to its urn.

Into the grave, with shouts of mirth,
We'll lay the treasured old one down,
And ring the bells of this great town,
And merry make on every hearth.

And when we've revelled till we're sore,
We'll then commence another year
With many a hope and many a fear,
The same as we have done before.

THE POISONED CUP.

TAKE it away, ye hypocrites,
   I will not drink it up;
The draught is from the depth of hell,
   There's poison in the cup.
Away, ye girning hypocrites,
   Why do ye friendship feign?
Think you I see not on your brows
   The mark God put on Cain?

With death your cup is pregnant aye,
   And though it may taste sweet,
I know the bane of such a draught,
   For man it was not meet.
Away with it, ye hypocrites,
   Ye instruments of pain;
Think you I see not on your brows
   The mark God put on Cain?

Take it away, ye hypocrites,
   Ye narrow-minded slaves;
By such as you the noblest men
   Are soon reduced to knaves.
In friendship's name, why offer me
   A cup that doth contain
A draught so bitter? drink of it
   None can, and laugh at pain.

Away with it, ye hypocrites,
  Betrayers of your kind ;
Ye withered reeds that nod assent
  To every breath of wind.
Where'er you tread corruption springs,
  There's woe aye in your train,
And brows that bear the fatal mark,
  The mark God put on Cain.

KISSES.

Of kisses ye'll get many a score,
  When like ye I got plenty ;
And many a note wi' kisses in't
  The kimmers will ha'e sent ye.

The women folks sae winning are,
  Nae mortal can resist them ;
And many a time, believe me, lads,
  I ha'e been forced to kiss them.

Ne'er mind the carles that them misca',
  Be thou a noble seaman,
For every tar, in peace or war,
  Clings closely to the women.

They cheer us on and up the hill,
  To men they're guiding stars,
So take a Venus o' yer ain,
  Like that great planet Mars.

Now be advised to take a wife,
    I'm wae for thee wi' nane ;·
Ye wad, I'm shure, far better be,
    Than keepin' house your lane.

But mair at this time I'll no say,
    Lest I should gae ower far ;
Yet ye might gi'e the jades a kiss,
    And ne'er be aught the waur.

THE CRUCIFIXION.

AND Mary wept to see her Son
Led to the cross by furious men—
They little thought who He was then—
And crucified the holy One.

Oh, pity, down the curtains draw,
And hide the sad scene if thou wilt ;
For guilty men His blood was spilt,
But, dying thus, fulfilled the law.

Between two thieves they nailed Him up,
And cast lots for His very clothes ;
Though at His word the dead arose,
He had to drink Himself that cup

Which all must drink of woman born :
The Son of God was not exempt,
Reviled and treated with contempt,
And held by learned scribes in scorn.

When down in death He leaned His head,
The skies grew dark, the mountains shook,   ·
And nature wore her saddest look,
When back to God His spirit fled.

THE SABBATH DAY.

Ho ! come with me unto the hills away,
On this the seventh, the sweet Sabbath day ;
For ever sacred to the human breast,
A day of adoration and of rest.

My church this mountain, and the things I see
Uplift my soul, O Lord, from earth to Thee,
Who walked upon the ocean, calmed the storm,
And wore awhile man's feeble fleshly form.

That glorious sun, on which all life relies,
Obedient to Thy will doth set and rise ;
Thy word made all things, and those stars which shine
Have on their brow Thy autograph divine.

Thy omniscience on all around appears,
And summer now her greenest vesture wears ;
Go where I may, or cast my wond'ring eyes,
My soul, O Lord, to Thee doth upward rise.

Upon this hill no narrow house of stone ;
Far from dull sermons and the organ's groan
I worship Thee, Thou great Mysterious Power,
Who formed each leaf and beautified each flower.

Here on the mountains—out of nothing made
By Thee who walked with Adam in the shade,
And spoke to Moses from the bush on fire—
I here can worship Thee as I desire.

What need I care what critics think or say
Of this my poem, written here to-day?
The better day, 'tis said, the better deed;
The book of nature I at all times read.

Within the world, O Lord, I feel and see
The many things which speak of heaven and Thee;
Far from the town 'tis pleasant here to stray,
And spend with nature the sweet Sabbath day.

THE YARROW HERD.

Rowed in his plaidie, my ain shepherd laddie,
   Hied him awa', 'mid the wild drivin' snaw;
In the glens o' Yarrow, frae me he did tarry,
   But again, my dear Jamie, I never mair saw.

I feared me that something had happened my Jamie,
   When back frae the hill came his doggie alane;
It look't in my face, and it whined often to me,
   And the pitifu' whine tell't me Jamie was gane.

Restless it wandered, baith oot and in dandered,
   For a moment the poor thing could never be still;
Like me, 'twas in sorrow, and on the next morrow
   It searched for its maister and whined on the hill.

Rowed in his plaidie, my ain shepherd laddie
  Lay stiff and cauld, 'neath the white snaw, asleep ;
O'er him the wind sighin'—at hame I was cryin'—
  Lost in the wild drift while tending his sheep.

Leal neighbours me pitied, and searched a' the hillside,
  But nane o' them a' my Jamie could find ;
I knew he had perished, sae dear and sae cherished,
  Sae I couldna but think that the fates were unkind.

By fair winding Yarrow, that famed stream o' sorrow,
  I searched for my laddie in utter despair,
And thought o' that maiden, like me sorrow laden,
  Who searched for her true love, by foemen slain there.

The fierce storm relented, and neighbours consented
  Once more in quest o' my Jamie to go ;
Rowed in his plaidie, they found my dear laddie,
  Cold, stiff, and dead, by that weird stream of woe.

MY FAITHER'S FIRESIDE.

'Tis not within yon castle fair that happiness can dwell,
With servants running to and fro attending every bell ;
Nor is it on the battle-field, where man encounters man,
And cuts in twa the slender threads of life's wee
    chequered span :
No, but within my Faither's house both love and peace
    abide,
And in it, too, a' tribes sit doon, and 'gree at His fireside.

'Tis not within the billiard room, nor yet within the bar,
Nor is it in yon palace great, where none but nobles are;
Nor is it in the chamber of some haughty crownéd head,
That has army against army to death or glory led:
No, but within my Faither's house both love and peace
    abide,
And in it, too, a' tribes sit doon, and 'gree at His fireside.

'Tis not within the banquet hall, nor yet in princely court,
Nor is it in the gay saloon of fashion's proud resort;
Nor is it on the feathered couch of indolence and ease,
Nor is it on the billows of the fathomless seas:
No, but 'tis in the heart's recess, exempt frae pomp and
    pride,
Wi' Him who opened up the way through death to that
    fireside.

'Tis not the bright allurements of pleasure's fairy ring
That can the balm of sweet content unto our bosoms
    bring;
No, frae a grander source than that the fount o' bliss
    must rise,
For in that life ayont the grave, 'tis there the secret lies;
Sae let us trust in Him who died for us, and aye confide,
And may a' mankind yet doonsit wi' Him at that fireside,

Where care and sorrow never come, nor tears the eyes
    make dim,
So let us strive to reach the door that's opened been by
    Him;

We needna fear to gang the gait that He Himself has
  trod,
Wi' a' our sins upon Him laid, a dire, oppressive load ;
And wi' Him, in that glorious hame, at last may a' abide,
For my Faither makes a' welcome that come to His
  fireside.

~~~~~~~~~~~

THE CANTIE FOLK O' BOWMONTSIDE.

GAE east or west, or where ye may,
  Within this world sae lang and wide,
Nae cantier folk in it ye'll find
    Than those upon the Bowmontside,
      The cantie folk o' Bowmontside,
      The kindly folk o' Bowmontside.

O' a' the folk I ever met
  Within this world sae lang and wide,
I'll gi'e my aith, as shure as daith,
    There's nane like those on Bowmontside,
      The cantie folk o' Bowmontside,
      The kindly folk o' Bowmontside.

Some may ha'e mair o' fortune's trash,
  And in far grander houses bide ;
But lack o' siller gi'es nae fash
    Unto the folk o' Bowmontside.
      The cantie folk o' Bowmontside,
      The kindly folk o' Bowmontside.

The hills are green, and pure the streams
  That through the glens o' Bowmont glide,
And byegone visions fill my dreams—
  The dreams I've had on Bowmontside—
    The cantie folk o' Bowmontside,
    The kindly folk o' Bowmontside.

May heaven deign to bless their lot,
  And sweet content o'er them preside;
And health and wealth attend each cot
  That reeks upon the Bowmontside—
    The cantie folk o' Bowmontside,
    The kindly folk o' Bowmontside.

I WEARY FOR THE SIMMER.

Oh, I weary for the simmer,
  Wi' its flowers on ilka plain,
For I hate the gloomy winter
  Wi' his cauld big draps o' rain;

For the sun is aye sae cheerless,
  And the woodlands look sae bare;
Oh, I long to hear the blackbird
  And the mavis sing ance mair.

I wish I saw the simmer,
  And the craik amid the hay,
And the lambkins rinnin' races
  O'er the daisy-speckled brae.

I weary for the simmer,
  Wi' its treasure-laden bees,
And canty cushats cooin'
  Round their nests upon the trees.

I weary for the simmer
  That the cuckoo ushers in ;
I long to see the brier rose
  And blossom o' the whin.

The butterfly I fain would see
  Gae sportin' o'er the plain ;
I wish I heard the lav'rock
  And the lintie sing again.

I wish I saw the simmer,
  And the kye upon the lea,
And rosy cheekit maidens
  Sittin' milkin' them wi' glee.

The air would then be balmy,
  And bees would cheerie hum
While preein' a' the blossoms
  O' that flowery time to come.

THE AULD LAIRD.

ON marriage bent, the auld laird said,
  " Gae saddle Dick to me,
For Jean's the fairest that I ken,
  And her I e'en maun see.

But Jeannie thought that youth and age
    Could never happy sail ;
And, like a dog, she sent him hame,
    Wi' shangie at its tail.

Wee Cupid in her dark eyes stood,
    With arrows round him slung,
And hearts of lovers at her back
    In countless numbers hung ;
The sunbeams in her tresses hid.
    Frae zephyrs scented sweet,
And gowans on the verdant plain
    Their bloom gave to her feet.

The wealthy laird within his ha'
    In secret oft did sigh,
And wondered how the lassie could
    His proffered suit deny ;
But out the truth I'll ha'e to bring—
    She lo'ed young Jamie best ;
And sae, for weel or woe, has made
    With him a cosy nest.

NEW YEAR'S DAY.

O'ER geese and turkeys some carouse
    And a' that's good and grand,
While others cannot e'en afford
    A herring on the brand ;

So ye that ha'e the poor folk mind,
　　Send something in their way—
A tate o' meal, a pickle coals,
　　Will help their New Year's Day.

It's drawin' near, 'twill soon be here,
　　And some ha'e nought to eat—
In idle groups, of ten and twelve,
　　They stand in many a street ;
In wealthy domes they hear the shout
　　Of children's happy glee,
And think upon their own at home
　　Wi' nought to haud it wi'.

It's drawin' near, 'twill soon be here,
　　And tables groan wi' fare ;
But, oh ! the rich can never ken
　　The hardships o' the puir ;
Sae ye that ha'e them something gi'e
　　To drive the wolf away,
For at the door of many a ane
　　He'll stand this New Year's Day.

And ere it comes I'd have you mind
　　The sad neglected puir,
Wha churchmen ever leave unto
　　Kind Providence's care ;
Let generous deeds your actions mark,
　　Nor grudge to give away
A little to your fellow men
　　This coming New Year's Day.

WEE TOMMY.

AROUND him the beautiful daisies,
  In churchyards they aye fairest grow ;
But the blossom we love and reverest
  Is lying the green sward below.

Last year the wee laddie plucked
  The daisies that now round him bloom ;
And little we thought they would garnish
  His bed in the lone silent tomb.

And much do we miss the wee laddie,
  That out to the garden would rin
For a handful of pretty white daisies,
  And crouse with them he would come in.

And oft would his kind mother chide him
  For culling the daisies so white,
Ne'er dreaming that they round his ashes
  In blossom so fair would unite.

So we cannot but love the sweet daisies,
  And wherever I see them in bloom
I remember wee Tommy that's lying
  Amid them, asleep in the tomb.

THE NEW YEAR.

THE new year comes, and I maun screw
  My fiddle up again,

And though the theme's been often sung,
   'Tis worthy o' a strain;
Then, lads and lasses, join your hands,
   And of it merry sing,
And may it nought but blessings to
   The race o' mankind bring.

This is the last day o' the year,
   And when the new is born,
A song of gladness shall arise
   To hail the happy morn.
Then, lads and lasses, join your hands,
   And form a social ring;
O'er a' the earth, on every hearth,
   May bliss extend her wing.

The bairns are wearyin' for it sair,
   And languish for the bun,
While older youths look forward to
   The whisky and the fun.
Then, lads and lasses, join your hands,
   And form a social ring;
With rapture hail the coming year,
   And of it merry sing.

The new year comes, and lasses blythe
   For it up spruce their hair,
And wonder oft wha will them take
   To trip it o'er the flair.

Then lads o' lasses mindfu' be,
  And let them ha'e a reel;
The cup o' bliss may a' men taste,
  And purest rapture feel.

Wi' me just picture to yourselves
  The pleasure that it brings;
Like Noah's dove the new year comes
  Wi' joy upon its wings.
Then, lads and lasses, join your hands,
  And onward merry steer,
And may a' foemen do the same
  Within the comin' year.

JEAN'S LAMENT.

O SIGH, ye winds of autumn, sigh,
  And wail upon the lea,
For I ha'e lost my ain auld man,
  The best of men to me.

He won my heart when I was young,
  But that is long ago,
When life's strange cup held nought but sweets,
  And seemed to overflow.

Through blinding tears I backward gaze
  Unto those pleasant hours,
When he within my tresses twined
  The pretty new-blown flowers.

My tresses then luxuriant were,
 Unlike what they are noo ;
The hue o' youth was on my cheek,
 And sunshine on my broo.

I then was happy as a bird
 Within its little nest,
For I had a' this world could gi'e,
 The man I likit best.

His like I never yet beheld,
 For he was aye sae crouse,
And wantin' him I weary sair
 In this auld theekit house,

Whose wa's are maist as frail's mysel'.
 And when death comes for me,
I hope to meet my auld guidman
 Where nae sad partings be.

STILL I MISS ONE.

Oft do I count with care my flock,
 Still I miss one ;
And ere I know, down o'er my cheeks
 The warm tears run.

In dreams upon my bed I see
 The one that's dead ;
How fondly, then, I kiss his cheek,
 And smooth his head.

In visions oft I see him walk
　　Across the floor,
Where he, alas ! my little man,
　　Shall walk no more ;

For he is laid beneath the sod,
　　In lasting rest,
And ne'er again shall he repose
　　On this, my breast.

But on the Saviour's he reclines
　　Both night and day,
And from His bosom none can take
　　My child away.

AULD COINS.

HECH, mony a pouch ye'll ha'e been in,
　　And mony a queer thing ye'll ha'e bought ;
Though unco lang ye've been concealed,
　　Again to use by chance ye're brought.

Was he a miser that you hid
　　In feudal times when raids were rife ?
For misers, for the sake of gold,
　　Would drain the very springs of life.

Whoe'er he was that hid you here,
　　I do not know, and little care ;
No doubt but you've provided cheer
　　For many a one at race or fair.

When I you found deep in the earth,
 I thought, no doubt, I'd wealth galore ;
Glum poverty forsook my hearth,
 And smiling friends besieged my door.

The parson kindly shook my hand,
 And others that you would not think ;
Nae lack of friends if ye but ha'e
 The name o' ha'ein' plenty clink.

To parties I was taken out,
 And mixed with all the great and gay ;
But from me now they've wheeled about,
 Because my siller's a' away.

WILLIE'S FAR FRAE BOWMONT.

Though spring may clothe ilk naked tree,
How changed the Bowmont seems to me ;
Ah, hush, ye birds, your strains o' glee,
 My Willie's far frae Bowmont.

Ye hills around the Border wide,
Wi' clouds o' grief your summits hide,
And backward flow, thou merry tide,
 My Willie's far frae Bowmont.

Adown the vale the river rins—
The linnet sings amang the whins ;
And speckled trout, with nimble fins,
 Sport in the stream o' Bowmont.

But sport for me, alas! there's nane,
For my true love awa' has gane,
And left me here my weary lane,
   Within the vale o' Bowmont.

With tears my cheeks are never dry,
And frae my bosom steals the sigh ;
Oh ! leave, thou lark, your song on high,
   For Willie's far frae Bowmont.

Oh, soothe, ye powers, my aching breast,
The soul within can find no rest ;
And like a bird, wi' ruined nest,
   I grieve and pine by Bowmont.

Oh, land of beauty, lore, and mist,
The last time that I Willie kiss't,
I little thought that he would list,
   And leave me thus by Bowmont.

By stream of streams I sit and lave
My burning brow, and here I rave ;
To me, 'twas here that Willie gave
   The heart that's far frae Bowmont.

Though fairy spring has clothed ilk tree,
And flowerets feast with sweets the bee,
There's nought but care and grief for me,
   For Willie's far frae Bowmont.

MY AULD FRIENDS.

My auld friends and loved friends are wearin' awa',
Like icicles in sunshine or snaw in a thaw ;
Like leaves on the ocean, propelled by the wave,
They are borne to that land, the land 'yont the grave.

How many I miss when backward I cast
Mine eyes, and behold the times that ha'e passed ;
I reckon them up, till lost in a maze,
And exclaim with the Psalmist, How short are our days !

O'er changes I've seen in Bowmont's fair vale
I pause and I ponder, I weep and I wail ;
Tongues that have charmed me are now mute and still
In the silent churchyard at foot o' the hill.

There lies the doctor, the learned old seer,
Who pleased me with stories, both ancient and queer ;
I have sat by his fire, and heard him rehearse
Far more than I ever could weave into verse.

His heart was fu' tender, though his manner was rude,
There was something about him excellingly good ;
He was true to his friends at home and abroad,
And a stauncher old Whig the earth never trod.

The houses he cherished to others are sold,
And the wife that survived him lies under the mould ;
Poor bodie, I've seen her, both early and late,
Whilst going my rounds, within the town gate.

She had aye something new ilk time me to tell,
Frae Adam the first to the last one that fell :
What events they recal, and round me entwine
The threads o' the braw days I've witnessed lang syne.

THE BRIER BUSH.

OH, I never saw a breer
    That I thought sae little o',
And were it no' the auld bush
    That blossomed long ago
I couldna sing as I sing noo,
    Though weel I like the strain,
For we'll never see a breer
    Like the auld bush again.

Oh, it doesna scent the breezes
    That through the woodlands blaw ;
The bush that charmed our hearts lang syne
    Had blossoms white as snaw :
The word o't touches nae the heart,
    And it's no' to be compared
Wi' the " bonnie, bonnie breer bush
    In oor kailyaird."

THE WHITE STEEDS.

I LOOKED up the valley, and, lo, in array,
The white steeds of ether were pawing the day—

Their manes, the high mountains, all covered with snow,
And their tails, the broad valleys, with lustre aglow.

Behind them fierce Boreas, with crystal-like reins,
Aguiding his chargers o'er the aërial plains ;
His chariot a storm-cloud, his kingdom all space,
And the wild heaving ocean reflected his face.

From the hoofs of the coursers arose such a drift
That it darkened old Phœbus that shone in the lift ;
They capered and reared up, and, lo, there came down
A thick shower of snowflakes all over the town.

Boys them gathered, and pelted the girls,
Who startled the echoes with loud merry skirls ;
The white steeds they galloped, and dashed on thro' air,
In their fetlocks and manes not a single brown hair :

In harness full mounted, with sun, moon, and stars,
With storm fiends upon them, they cleared the high bars ;
Behind them King Boreas, defiant and proud,
The lord of the winter, his mantle a cloud,

With a cold polar ray in his hand for a whip,
Which none but himself would have courage to grip,
He urged on his steeds, as if running a race,
And the storm fiends of ether enjoyed the chase.

The snow clouds they trampled and scattered about—
"Oh, that terrible snow," the people would shout,
"It falls, and has fallen, as never before,
And the storm fiends with howling are wearied and sore."

For three days and three nights the chargers have run,
And he laughs at the mischief the white steeds have
    done ;
His chariot, with arched necks, they proudly it drew,
On the pinions of winter storms after it flew.

From region to region they bounded along,
And each fiend in his hand held an icicle thong ;
I viewed them with wonder, and this I did say,
" The white steeds of ether have galloped this day."

SERGEANT READDIE, LATE OF JEDBURGH.

Oн, death, thou art an unco carl,
What ailed thee at puir Davie ?
At forty-eight, 'twas rather sune,
   To play him such a shavie ;
His heart aye beat abune a' cares,
And though he fell at times in snares,
   Aye up again rose Davie.

Wi' kilt 'bune knee, in the Crimea,
   Ayont the ocean wavy,
Where shot and shell the thickest fell,
   Wi' sword in hand was Davie.
A braver soldier ne'er drew breath,
But now he's cold and still in death,
   And a' lament for Davie.

M

On Inkerman's blood-crimsoned height,
  'Mid hazards oft and shavie,
Like Samson, he our foes did smite,
  Sae valorous was Davie ;
But, lack-a-day ! the bravest must
Some time or other bite the dust,
  For in the mould is Davie.

Achilles, born of goddess fair,
  Ne'er did the deed he would not dare ;
The clasps and medals he did wear,
  Were dearly won by Davie :
Where champing chargers dash amain,
And blood in streams ooz'd frae the slain,
  There they were won by Davie.

Wherever fell the rudest shock,
  There stood he firm as granite rock ;
And, oh ! his croon got many a knock,
  For scaur on scaur had Davie ;
But death at last has laid him doon,
Nae mair he'll see yon siller moon,
  For in the dust lies Davie.

On Alma, where brave Campbell drew
  His Highlanders in line of two,
Before a hostile Russian crew,
  None forward marched like Davie ;
And when Sebastopol did fall
Who mounted first the battered wall ?
  No other than poor Davie.

At Lucknow, where a tawny race
  On noble Britons heap'd disgrace,
None bolder did the Sepoys face,
  At bayonet's point, than Davie :
The bagpipes o' the Campbells brought
Relief to those who long it sought,
  And in their van was Davie.

To Davie now let's say fareweel ;
  For those bereft we deeply feel,
And we shall do our best to heal
  The hearts that bleed for Davie :
Those near and dear his care will miss,
But He who tends the fatherless
  Will guard those left by Davie.

ADIEU, MY FRIEND.

Adieu, my friend ! and though 'tis hard to part,
I wish thee well wherever thou may'st be.
Know this : thou hast a corner of my heart,
A sterling friend thou'st been to more than me,
And many a muse shall mourn when reft of thee,
My generous patron, on the fairy Jed ;
In doleful numbers now we all may sing
For one who oft us with indulgence fed,
And taught us how to soar upon the wing.
O'er me, Apollo, come, thy mantle fling,
A sonnet to my patron let me weave ;
Ye winds that through the leafless woodlands moan,
To you, depress'd, I listen and I grieve,
Because the friend I loved has from me gone.

The hill of life, they say, 'tis ill to climb,
And up it, friend, I'm glad to see thee rise :
Thy cup with sweets be filled up to the brim,
Well hast thou run, long wear the golden prize ;
Serene and cloudless ever be your skies,
From all that's gloomy may they still be clear,
And health attend thee wheresoe'er thou tread.
God guide thy footsteps in a higher sphere,
And sweet contentment soothe thy path a-head,
And all thy journey be with roses spread.
In fancy let me clasp thy helpful hand,
And wring it warmly while my cheeks are wet ;
Still by the weak a mighty pillar stand :
Farewell, my friend ! you go, and I regret.

My friend, farewell ! since Fate calls thee away,
I have a tear, and do not grudge it you ;
To meet again I hope, but never may ;
Such souls as thine are far between and few ;
As ivy round the tree our friendship grew,
But wanting thee I flounder on forlorn.
With kindness thou my spirit to thee drew ;
This tribute take, my friend, it do not scorn,
Tho' from a heart with its own throbbings worn,
For in my spring of life it beat right bold.
In Edina have thee ever great success,
And Fortune never look upon thee cold ;
The Giver of all good with goodness bless
Thyself and family—heaven grant thee this.

A MOTHER'S FLOWER.

A MOTHER's flower, and father's too,
    Within the mould lies there ;
That little spot of hallowed earth,
    May ruthless man it spare.

For in it lies the dust of one
    For ever from them taken,
And oft they gaze upon that spot
    Which in their minds awaken

The memories of other days,
    When they pure pleasure tasted ;
But fragile flowers in early spring
    Are more than easy wasted.

For Boreas came, and shrivelled up
    The petals of that flower,
Tho' strange, 'tis true, the hopes of men
    Oft perish in an hour.

They say that time can heal all wounds,
    And drought all fountains dry—
It may be so, but still the tears
    Of sorrow dim the eye.

AULD GEORDIE.

NAE mair in the Kirkwynd nor Loan shall we see him,
Nae mair on the Rule nor by Teviot he'll tread,

And sorry were we in the graveyard to leave him,
   A canty auld bodie was Geordie that's dead.

Nae mair shall he lead us, as oft he has led us,
   And weel may we sprinkle wi' tears a' the Loan;
He was e'en a freen' and guid lawyer to us,
   And sair we miss Geordie that's from us a' gone.

Nae mair to the huntin' shall Geordie gae wi' us,
   Tho' oft o'er the mountains he us to it led;
He was a queer bodie, and kind he was to us,
   And a' that e'er kent him are wae that he's dead.

Unmolested the maukins may feed on the stibble
   And dae as they like, for never shall he
Catch them again as they come out to nibble
   The sweet blades o' verdure on hillside or lea.

Tho' ithers may try it by netting or gunning,
   Wi' Geordie the best o' us couldna compare;
He went aye aboot it sae pawky and cunning,
   And never gaed oot but he brought hame a hare.

Auld " Heather " may blaw o' his muckle daein's
   When drinkin' a drap wi' a cronie or twa,
But what need we care for his half muddled sayin's?
   For he never could catch them like him that's awa'.

Fareweel to Geordie, nae mair shall we see him
   In Howgate, the Foreraw, the Kirkwynd, or Loan;
His dougie, puir creature, seems dowie without him,
   And a' folk that kent him are wae that he's gone.

TOM BROWN.

THE winds round the mountains of Teviotdale sigh,
    And sullen December is draigled wi' rain,
And warm tears are streamin' frae mony an eye,
    For Tammas, puir bodie, for ever is gane.

Now that he's departed, and left us a' dreary,
    If faults he had ony we'll lichtly them scan,
For wantin' the auld cock, we canna but weary,
    And lang we'll remember the decent auld man.

Good men and bad men are destined to perish,
    And Tammas, auld Tammas, in death he's asleep ;
Sacred for ever, his shade let us cherish,
    Though with mirth the proud maukins his wake did
        it keep.

The winds round the mountains of Teviotdale sigh,
    And down in the woodlands the cushats complain,
And warm tears are streamin' frae mony an eye,
    For Tammas o' Howgate that's now frae us gane.

HEATHER JOCK.

O COME, my muse, with sorrow come,
    And view the grave o' Heather Jock ;
His faults and failings let us fling
    Into oblivion's mighty pock.

His place of death befitted well
 The wretched life the creature led,
And tender pity makes one feel
 While gazing on his humble bed.

In life his friends were cold and few,
 His daily bread was often scant;
But this or that he'll need from none,
 He's now beyond the reach of want.

Crane-like he watched the purling streams,
 And for a crust would gather bones;
Of statute laws he's broken more
 Than ere he broke of hard whin stones.

Yet in our memory he dwells,
 And though his end the muse may shock,
On Hawick streets no more we'll see
 The jaded form of Heather Jock.

SCOTLAND.

The splendour of my country never shall grow dim,
The greenness of her laurels cannot fade;
Her frowning mountains and her flowery dales
Are shrined in songs of love and tales of war.
The sword of Wallace and the spear of Bruce
Are sheathed in everlasting patriot fame.
Who have not felt the blood within them stir
When conning o'er the deeds of those great men?

They hewed our freedom out of tyrants' crowns,
And put their foes to ignominious flight ;
But for such heroes, what had we now been ?
A conquered people ; but our thistle waves :
Despite of all that ever yet assayed
To crush it down, ever it rose in strength.
Long may it blossom on the storied soil
Of dear old Scotland, mother of the brave !
On Cartland's Crags oft have I mused alone,
Conjuring up the deeds of her bold chief,
For there " Blind Harry " tells us he did hide,
And, lion-like, spring out upon his foes
Who slew his wife, and with his mighty sword
From thraldom freed the country that him sold.
Oh, false Monteith ! if Harry's tale be true,
It is enough to make all Scotsmen blush.
And, cruel Edward, couldst thou not have spared
The only man who never bent to thee ?
Dark be the end of those who would betray
The land where freedom's beak first broke the shell
Of serfdom's egg, dropt in a nest of chains.
With German princes I would not exchange
One drop of Teviot for half of their Rhine.
In thee, old Scotland, I first saw the light
Of that proud April sun within the west ;
And while I live I'll ever cling to thee,
My native land, of every land the pride.

WHO IS HE?

Who is he within our city, talking French and Latin
    lore ?
He's the master of ten languages, and some say even
    more.
Oh ! my brain whirls with amazement as the hero comes
    in sight,
For his eyes are full of language that no common bard
    can write.

See him walk along the passage of that great and gor-
    geous hall,
Stopping now to write in shorthand the requests of one
    and all,
Light as any roebuck skipping o'er the heather in full
    bloom,
Leaping up the stairs like lightning, to and fro from
    room to room.

Could I paint this man of letters I would make him
    such a peer,
For he is the prince of brandies, and the king of stoutest
    beer ;
There's a grandeur in his features and a swiftness in his
    tread,
And he wears the crown of learning full of jewels on
    his head.

Who is he ? a mighty genius, climbing up the rocks of
    life,
With a glory all around him—in his hand a loaf and
    knife,
Giving bread to all that hunger—mark his lip and mark
    his mein,
These of noble cast, the rarest in our city ever seen.

He will bring you draughts of comfort if you only but
    him tell,
And can give you all the history of the happy pair who
    fell—
E'en the world from the beginning all its mystery can
    explore,
And he'll open up discussions that you never heard
    before.

Travellers smile to see him with a sirloin of good beef
On a salver decorated with many a pretty leaf ;
He reminds me of a diamond that a Persian lady found,
Sparkling in the depth of night, upon the pitchy ground ;

Or, like a rose 'mong bushes of thorns and brambles
    twined,
Shedding upon all the fragrance of his great and giant
    mind.
Who is he, this man of wonders ? Oh, the question ask
    no more—
He's the Titian of all scholars, speaking languages
    galore.

THE BUTTERFLIES.

In Liddesdale, where winter lies,
And very rarely ever dies,
I saw a pair of butterflies,
   Like lad and lass,
Together where the plover cries,
   'Mid bent and grass.

No tint of green nor flower was there
To charm the happy flaunting pair ;
On Liddesdale, so bleak and bare,
   No signs of spring,
Excepting these, beyond compare,
   Upon the wing.

From whence came they ? methought or said,
And so to musing I was led ;
Upon the hills the flocks were spread
   In fleecy pride—
A grander scene I never spied
   On Liddleside.

A cold keen breeze came o'er the hill,
Enough the tiny things to kill ;
Close by a stream or winding rill,
   Like crystal clear,
Those pretty insects roved at will,
   The first this year.

So may not man who lives and dies,
In the eternal spring arise
Rechanged, and in another guise,
   On that fair shore ?
For were not those gay butterflies
   Just worms before ?

S P R I N G.

SPRING in her robes o' green,
Fair as a fairy queen,
With blossoms returneth
   Again in her breast.
Birds hail her coming,
More sweet than the humming
Of poets that plague her
   With rhymes not the best.

From her rich tresses flinging
The sunbeams there hinging,
Like maiden the fairest,
   Both comely and sweet.
She cheers us and charms us,
Delighteth and warms us,
And wee pretty gowans
   Smile under her feet.

She treads on them lightly,
Her touch makes them sprightly,

And her breath sends a thrill
　Through the bare blighted trees.
Flowers round her sunny brow,
Snowdrops and crocus now
Tell us she's coming
　From over the seas.

Soft winds are blowing,
With health her cheeks glowing,
High o'er the mountains
　The lark's piping clear,
Poised in the chilly air,
Hailing that maiden fair
Whom we all cherish,
　Esteem, and revere.

By Jed she doth wander
In all her rare grandeur ;
The fair lovely maiden,
　Her praise I will sing.
Fairer there cannot be,
Birds perched on bush and tree
Pour out their ditties
　To welcome the spring.

THE BEAUTIFUL SPRING.

THE beautiful spring, like an infant kissed,
　Reopened her eyes, and smiled through showers
Which have given earth a vigour and zest
　To bring us back the fragrant flowers.

On her delicate feet the dewdrops lie,
    Which shimmer and gleam as the morning sun
With his chariot of gold illumes the sky,
    And clothes the woods with a brilliant dun.

But, remember this, that her reign is brief,
    And from us all, like a shadow, she'll pass ;
Yet her fairy fingers formeth the leaf,
    And with curious scissors shapeth the grass.

Wherever she setteth her fair feet down,
    A rich greenness under them up doth arise,
And her breath brings health to the pent-up town,
    Where the curse of Eden ever lies.

From the crowded slums of miniature hells,
    Come, come, let us haste to the distant wild,
And breathe the air of the lofty fells
    From the fanners of heaven undefiled.

Hark ! listen ! the birds down in yonder break,
    How charmingly sweet their sweet notes ring,
And the ducks, 'mid the sedges of that broad lake,
    Are happy and crouse because it is spring ;

For the beautiful maid all nature charms,
    And the croaking frogs in their dreamy pools
Swim here and there with their dears in their arms,
    For the spring the great heart of nature rules.

I MISS HER.

I miss her ! oh, I miss her !
   Sae altered is the house,
It's no the same since she has left,
   That had a smile sae crouse.
I miss the bonnie lassie
   That was aye sae blythe and free,
And wantin' her, what is this world ?
   A desert place to me.

I miss her ! oh, I miss her !
   For she had sae muckle mirth,
There's no' another half sae fair
   And charming on this earth.
When I came frae my daily work,
   O'ercome wi' care an' toil,
She never failed to glad me wi'
   A cheery, pleasant smile.

I miss her ! oh, I miss her !
   And there's nane to pity me ;
Though her mither, puir auld body,
   Gi'es me whiles a cup o' tea,
And makes me aye as welcome
   As ever to the house,
Where I miss the bonnie lassie
   That was aye sae clean and crouse.

THE WATERS OF LOVE.

I've tasted the waters of love's purest spring,
    And bask'd in the sunshine of purest delight ;
I thought that those moments would never take wing :
    But as meteors they vanished and fled from my sight.

In childhood I wandered beside a clear stream
    That flowed through a meadow bespangled with
        flowers ;
And there I of manhood indulged in a dream—
    A dream fraught with visions of youth's sunny hours.

As time rolled along on his great restless car,
    My bright sun grew dimmer—his rays, pale and wan,
Gave way to the evening of manhood's first star,
    And too soon I felt all the cares of a man.

Fate upraised the finger, and, pointing, said, " Go,
    Go where I bid thee, and go with good cheer,
Thy life's but a stream, and howe'er it may flow,
    In eternity's gulf it will soon disappear."

Since then I have wandered in paths strewed with
        thorns,
    But amongst them sweet blossoms appeared here and
        there ;
The roughest of pathways some floweret adorns,
    And brightens the aspect of dark-eyed despair.

N

Our life has real joys if we could them but see,
    For clouds are not ever obscuring the skies ;
The song of the mavis, the hum of the bee,
    Might teach us a lesson each morning we rise.

Oh, say not that life is encumbered with care,
    I tell you, if burdened, what will it remove :
From your breast cast the serpent that's lying coiled there,
    And take but one draught of the waters of love.

THE LINTIE.

THEY say I'm canty in my cage,
    And that I whistle cheery ;
Believe it not, 'tis all a hoax,
    For freedom still I weary.

I long to touch my native twig
    Upon yon bushy brae,
And sit amid the yellow broom
    With all my mates so gay.

What though my jailor's good and kind,
    And gives me food the best ?
He little thinks for what I pine,
    The grief that rends my breast.

And when he coaxes me to sing
    The song of memories glad,
The notes that please him bring to me
    An echo—ah ! how sad.

It minds me of the love I lost
　That bleak December morn,
When, hungry, to the farmyard here
　I came to peck the corn.

And if he'd let me fly once more
　Free o'er my native plain,
I'd fill the welkin, as of yore,
　With songs of gladder strain ;

No more by prison bars confined,
　I'd seek my downy nest,
And warble o'er the broomy knowes
　Which nature's hand has dressed.

THE YEARS OF MEN.

THE years of men pass on with ceaseless roll,
　For in this world there's no abiding place ;
Time wears all bodies, and the immortal soul,
　Bird-like, soon flies from out the shattered case.

Life's called a dream, but 'tis a dream which needs
　The whip and spur, and energy of will ;
The Jackal to his prey the Lion leads,
　Though he can neither capture it nor kill.

For daily bread all ranks are doomed to toil,
　And those who work not cannot hope to eat ;
Remember but the virgins void of oil—
　But this old story I need not repeat.

Be up and earnest in whate'er you do,
  Whether it be with shovel, pick, or pen ;
To others and yourselves be ever true,
  And act the parts allotted you like men.

This is no age for sluggards, and we feel
  The short-lived years fast from us glide away,
And sober night comes wrapped in her dark veil,
  So let us labour while we have the day ;

For soon the sun of twenty-one sinks down
  Behind the minarets of sixty years,
And when for ever they are from us flown,
  How like a dream long perish'd all appears.

In youth's bright days I took no note of time,
  And, minnow-like, I sported with the shoal
Of mankind in this ever changeful clime,
  Where mighty time doth all before him roll.

MARY M'LEOD, WILTON.

Long ere the autumn had blighted the roses
  That scented sae sweetly the garden and glade,
Mary—the fairest o' a' earthly posies—
  Under the mould in the churchyard was laid.

O' a' the sweet flowerets that bloomed in the simmer,
  The charms o' my Mary outrivalled them a' ;
But Death cast his e'e on the fairy-like kimmer—
  And sae he has ta'en her for ever awa'.

It makes me aye sad when I look roon' the ingle,
    And see nae my Mary—o' maidens the pride;
Nae mair shall her voice wi' the voices here mingle,
    And wantin' her, dowie appears the fire-side.

Fain wad I hae kept her frae Death's cauld embrace,
    But the will o' great Heaven we canna deny;
Amongst a' the angels there's nae sweeter face
    Than that o' my Mary, wi' Christ now on high.

Nae mair will she tread o'er the bonnie white daisies
    That speckle wi' blossom the green dewy glade;
Safe wi' her Saviour, and singing His praises,
    Naught but her garments are in the grave laid.

Tho' re-clothed in bright robes, and far frae a' sorrow,
    My heart it is lonely, and langs for her here;
But why should I murmur? she's better in glory—
    Yet wha could begrudge her a sigh or a tear?

Farewell to my Mary, nae mair shall I see her
    Amid her companions in woodland or street;
Still let me hope in that fair home to meet her—
    For the bitterest cup may have drops that are sweet.

LIEUTENANT SCOTT DOUGLAS.

In prime of life there was o'erthrown
    A hero brave and young,
And shall the heir of Springwood sleep
    In Zululand unsung?

No ! like his kin on fame's great roll,
    He sought a soldier's grave ;
And for his country nobly died
    Beyond the briny wave.

And Scotland mourns her hero slain,
    Of death he had no fear ;
Trained to the early use of arms
    Which he did proudly wear.

In battle dire he seemed at home,
    Of Douglases the chief ;
Now sleeping in a foreign land,
    Cut down in greenest leaf.

Far from the scenes he dearly loved
    His bones in earth are laid,
The lustre of his warlike race
    Shall ne'er grow dim nor fade.

And long shall Scotland mourn the loss
    Of Springwood's gallant James,
Now placed upon the mighty roll
    Of everlasting names.

THE WEATHER.

The weather, oh ! the weather,
    And the May-time tho' it be ;
The air is rather chilly yet
    For butterfly or bee.

But every thing is beautiful,
  In season and in space ;
And languid nature rises up
  Wi' health upon her face.

The weather, oh ! the weather,
  In the vernal month of May,
Impels the laverock frae the earth
  Unto the vaults of day ;

And there on joyous, outstretch'd wings,
  Wi' sunshine on his breast,
He whistles, till he seeks at eve
  His fair one on her nest.

The weather, oh ! the weather,
  Tho' it's lang been dull and grey,
The gowans smile on yonder plain,
  And kiss the lips o' May.

For in May the song-birds warble
  Their sweetest notes of love ;
And the woods are never silent
  With the amorous dove.

THE BLIGHTED ROSE.

THE fairest rose that ever grew
  Has blighted been in bloom ;
Now o'er the vale of classic Tweed
  Dark clouds of sorrow loom.

Without it bleak the vale appears,
   No more the summer dew
Shall sparkle on the petals that
   Were spotless in their hue.

That beauteous rose none can describe,
   The fairest of all flowers,
Has been removed, and planted in
   A fairer clime than ours.

The Hand which culled it, though unseen,
   Still guides the fate of men ;
And why it was so early pluck'd
   Is hid from human ken.

We know 'twill bloom ayont the stars,
.   Which none but seers can read ;
And hope breaks through the cloud of gloom
   That's brooding been o'er Tweed.

Life at the best is but a gift,
   And He who it bestows
Has't in His power to take or give,
   And so He snatched the rose.

He saw it was too fair for earth,
   And lifted it on high,
And placed it safely in a vase
   Where it can never die.

THE MIDGE AND THE FLEE.

A PAMPERED midge said to a flee,
" Bow down, obey, and honour me ;"
The flee, amazed, began to fidge,
And thus replied unto the midge—

" How dare you thus set up your face ?
The meanest of the insect race
Shall never lord it over me,
Though I be nothing but a flee."

" Within some dunghill thou wert bred,
While I, while I," the proud midge said,
" Came from the blow of yon sweet thorn,
Kiss'd with the rosy lips of morn."

" Thou pompous thing," the flee replied,
" On me your pranks too long you've tried ;
And all my kind you've much tormentit,
And few you like if ye but kent it."

" Know this," the midge, offended, said,
" On helpless flees I like to tread ;
Though but the insect of a day,
O'er flees I reign with tyrant sway."

At this the flee paused on the pane—
" Some day shall end thy little reign ;
Though now you lord it over all,
Like Lucifer, you yet may fall.

"And if I may the plain truth tell,
A viler spirit never fell
From heaven to earth than what thou art ;
There's nought but evil in thy heart."

The midge, annoyéd with this speech,
Flew off from out the poor flee's reach ;
The flee him raxed upon the pane,
And said, "No midge shall o'er me reign.

"It was the midge this quarrel began,
For midges petty actions plan,
And work them out with traitor skill,
For in them there is nought but ill."

KINGS ON HIGH.

ADVERSE fate may overtake us,
Poverty make friends forsake us,
But the Lord hath said He'll make us
  Kings on high.

In Him trust, and do not weary,
Though life's path be rough and dreary ;
Onward march, steadfast and cheery,
  Till you die.

From every danger He can save us,
And in sorrow ne'er forsake us ;
After death, I know, He'll make us
  Kings on high.

Dearest friends they may deceive us,
Sons and daughters pain and grieve us,
But from such He will relieve us
    When we die.

Adverse fate may frown upon us,
Poverty make friends disown us,
But the Lord hath said He'll crown us
    Kings on high.

JOHN CAMPBELL, BAKER, HAWICK.

Scarce twenty-three when he was laid
    Beside the peaceful dead ;
Ah ! ne'er again shall stunted health
    Confine him to sick bed.

No, he is far beyond the pale
    Of sickness and disease ;
The sweetest flowers oft perish first,
    And he was one of these.

His like, indeed, we seldom see,
    So gentle and so mild ;
Resigned, he kissed the cup of death,
    With lips that ever smiled.

Now in a brighter world than this
    He rests his wearied head
Upon the breast of that great One
    Who for all mankind bled.

Then let us bid adieu to grief,
　And this our bosoms cheer—
Though parted now, we yet shall meet
　In that celestial sphere

Where rainbow colours ever glow
　And angels ever sing,
Who knows but he to that fair land
　Was borne on seraph's wing?

It may be fancy, but I think
　That he is happy there,
With Him who did the fall of man
　By His own death repair.

THE SNAIL.

To injure you I would be laith,
　So hide not thou thy horns frae me ;
The God that formed you gave me breath,
　So harm, my friend, I would not thee.

To some dyke back creep thou away,
　And keep thou off the turnpike road,
For in the mirk or morning grey
　Some one may hurt you, heavy shod.

Though snail thou be, I would not like
　To see you pressed into a jelly,
Nor wyndle strae put in your e'e
　By some hard-hearted, thoughtless fellow.

Some hate you for the trail you leave
  Upon whatever you've been crawlin';
Though ill it looks on some braw sleeve
  Of gown or coat from clothes-line fallen,

For that I'll never shun thee—nay,
  Nor blush to own you as a brither,
For God at first made man from clay,
  So earth must be of all the mither.

The waiblen jukes, beware o' them,
  For unco fast your kind they swallow ;
And if they here upon you come,
  About it long they would not dally.

Take my advice, creep off the road,
  Lest wheel of cart or carriage crush thee,
For east and west they ply abroad,
  So be you aye as well's I wish thee.

THE FLOWER O' KALE.

The sweetest flower I ever saw
  In blossom upon hill or dale,
It was a beauty, bloomin' braw,
  Upon the bonnie banks o' Kale.

Its form was tall, its stem was small,
  Should aught befa' it I would wail ;
Oh, were it mine—but it never shall,
  The pretty flower on the banks o' Kale.

It charmed my bosom to the core,
　Waving in the bleak spring gale;
Its like I never spied before
　In blossom on the banks o' Kale.

And long I gazed upon this flower,
　Brighter than bright peacock's tail;
With ling'ring look I left the bower
　Where grew the fairest flower o' Kale.

I'll mind unto my dying hour
　That matchless flowcret o' the vale,
And may no bitter autumn shower
　E'er blight it on the banks o' Kale.

THOMAS THOMSON,

LATE SHEPHERD, MELLENDEAN, SPROUSTON.

My friend, the shepherd, best of fellow-men,
　Has paid at last that debt by nature due;
To sing his praise, with grief I lift the pen—
　Upon his ashes sweetest incense strew.

His part is finished, and he played it well—
　The race is over, and 'twas nobly run;
Yon wide-spread flock at morn no more he'll tell,
　Nor carry home with pride the missing one.

That crook and plaid in life no more he'll need—
　No, Annie, no! but keep them for his sake;

And spare, O God ! the remnant of his seed,
    Whose hearts with sorrow now are like to break.

How still the tongue that once possessed the art
    Of making words in grandest music roll ;
Death never pierced, methinks, a kinder heart,
    From human breast ne'er fled a purer soul.

Poor Tyne, his dog, I hear it whine amain,
    For him it oft doth long and piteous wow ;
He's gone, and back he'll never come again—
    No, Annie, no ! he's far from Tweedside now.

Alas ! our days are chequered, few, and short ;
    But yesterday I saw him— to him spake,
His bright eyes sparkled, and his vigorous port
    Seemed full of health that nought could ever shake.

And yet 'tis true my good old friend is dead,
    But mourn I'll not o'er ashes 'neath the sod
In hope of an eternal life he died—
    Without a murmur, calmly kissed the rod.

In beauteous Kelso, fairest town on earth,
    His worth was known, and there 'twill oft be told :
No more we'll meet at Sprouston round his hearth
    At Handsel Monday, as in days of old.

No, Annie, no ! those times have flitted past,
    Just as the ripples of some rapid stream ;
Flowers bloom and fade, and trees their foliage cast—
    Oh ! what is life ? the shadow of a dream !

MY LITTLE LAMBIE.

Come awa', my little lambie,
 Toddle tentie, come to me;
Weel ye like to get a hobble
 On yer auld grandfaither's knee.

What wad I no' gi'e, my lambie,
 For my days o' happy youth,
Fled for ever—return never—
 Age is full of woe and ruth.

Come awa', my little lambie,
 Pat me on the cheek and broo;
Ance my cheeks were red and rosy,
 Though they're pale and withered noo.

Pat me on the auld bald croonie,
 Ance sae thick o' gouden hair;
Like a tree in bleak December,
 Stript o' a' its leaves sae bare.

Fast I'm sailin' down the river
 That ye ha'e been cast upon;
Will ye think upon grand-daddie,
 When I'm frae thee ever gone?

Will ye mind his auld white haffits,
 And the lowe that lit his e'e,
When ye was a wee, wee bairnie,
 Getting hobbles on his knee?

Twine yer arms about my neckie,
  Aye sae cantie, crouse, and fain ;
What wad I no' gi'e, my lambie,
  To be young as thee again ?

Fare ye weel, my little lambie,
  Aye sae merry may thou be ;
Life at best is but a hobble,
  Swift the days of mankind flee.

THE BARMAID.

FAIRER than her couldna be,
  Emblem of the richest blossom ;
Mercy, Cupid, sparest me,
  Bid her heal my wounded bosom.

Bring to me a jug of ale,
  Silly man is aye so stupid :
Who has not a victim been
  To the shafts of little Cupid ?

Fairer than the fairest floweret
  In the gardens of the great ;
And she'll bring you flowing measure
  Of good ale, like maid of state.

He that never saw that fair one,
  Let him come to Teviotdale,
For she is the sweetest maiden
  That e'er drew a pint of ale.

o

Fill a bumper, here's to Annie !
　Annie aye sae clean and crouse,
Wanting her the ale would perish—
　Maidens make or spoil a house.

Round her head a wreath of roses,
　In her hand a jug of ale,
In her breast the scented hawthorn,
　But all flowers before her´ pale.

PATIE.

Oh, mither, where is Patie noo ?
　We ne'er see him ava ;
Whisht, bairnies, whisht ! while frae her e'en
　Tears on the hearth-stane fa'.

And will he no come back again
　To romp wi' us and play ?
Whisht, bairnies, whisht ! ye little ken
　What foolish things ye say.

But, then, you told us he but slept,
　And when shall he awake ?
Whisht, bairnies, whisht ! for dae ye wish
　This heart o' mine should break ?

Oh, where did a' yon men him take
　That came here dressed in black ?
Whisht, bairnies, whisht ! and dinna sae
　Your mither's bosom rack.

But where did they wi' him gae to ?
  Oh, tell us if you can.
Whisht, bairnies, whisht ! in heaven noo
  Is Patie, ma wee man.

Bright angels met him at the gate,
  And bade him welcome in ;
Whisht, bairnies, whisht ! for never mair
  Shall he back to us win.

And who shall be his cronies there,
  Or kiss him when he cries ?
Whisht, bairnies, whisht ! nae bairnies greet
  When they are in the skies.

Wi' other bairnies like himsel',
  On streets of gold he'll play ;
Whisht, bairnies, whisht ! for who can tell
  The joys he there may ha'e

In that fair home wi' Him who died
  For a' upon the tree ?
Whisht, bairnies, whisht ! and ask nae mair
  About wee Pate at me.

THE DEID LICHT.

A HEAVY splash, and a weird-like cry,
  Startled the gloomy nicht ;
And I saw, and I saw on the water-side
  A fearsome kind o' licht.

And waukrife bodies that daunnert about
    The suburbs, out in the rain,
Heard a splash, and a weird-like cry,
    Again, again, and again.

The hair o' their heids upraise on end,
    And their flesh wi' awe did creep;
Oh! I doot, I doot there is something wrang—
    There is somebody into the deep.

And what is that on the water-side,
    Did ye ever see sic a sicht
In days of yore?   Often before—
    And I'll bet ye it's a deid licht.

Oh! gi'e me a grip o' yer waukit han',
    For I scarce can stan' my lane;
And did ye no' hear in the river the noo
    A splash like the splash o' a stane?

The river rows wi' an eerie soun'
    Abune and below the linn;
And close by the flood, near the leafless wud,
    A dog doth sit and whine.

Oh! what can ail that wee dowg ava,
    By the river-side thi' nicht;
I feel sae queer, and I gaze wi' fear
    On that flickerin', cauld, deid licht.

Oh ! there's something wrang, for I heard a splash,
  And then I heard a moan,
And wild Boreas stood in the heart o' the wood
  Spell-bound wi' a death-like groan.

Hame, oft hame, the wee dowgie ran,
  But aye returned to the stream,
And whined lang and sair by the very spot
  Where the cauld deid licht did gleam.

THE AULD FISH POOK.

THOUGH it was naething but a pock,
  For gowd it I'll no gi'e,
Because auld Heather it bequeathed
  A legacy to me;
My certie, lads, I may be prood,
  And up my bonnet cock,
For at his death he left to me
  The auld fish pock.

In it he carried many a fish
  Frae Teviot to the Loan;
The banes o' horses, sheep, and kye
  Been in it, many a stone.
He was a funny sort o' chiel,
  A queer ane, Heather Jock;
And antiquarians fain wad ha'e
  The auld fish pock.

About the toon wi' it he gaed
    For mony a weary year,
And wi't frae aff his cheek wad dicht
    The sorrow-speakin' tear ;
But it he'll carry never mair,
    For in the mould lies Jock,
And for his sake I'll ever keep
    The auld fish pock.

FICKLE FORTUNE.

WE cannot tell the cause of all
The ups and downs of this short life,
For changes come, and in the strife
We're overwhelmed by many a squall.

And some get wrecked upon the main,
Where many barques together sail ;
For few succeed, and thousands fail,
So ill is success to attain.

And, thinking on the cold rebuff
Of fickle fortune and her train,
A haze creeps o'er the tortured brain
Of him that smarteth from her cuff.

In quest of gold we onward ply
Through storm and sunshine everywhere,
To gather it, our only care ;
But fortune is a maiden shy.

And much we pity Samuel's case,
For once she led him by the hand ;
What castles then he built on sand,
But they have tumbled, and no trace

Of them appears, and where they stood
Thorns and nettles up have sprung,
And now the theme of many a tongue,
The jest of all the multitude.

And for him there be few that mourn :
Once rich and happy—now, alas !
The grains of luck have left his glass,
And back they never may return.

And they who once him homage paid,
No more receive him as their guest ;
They say he has become a pest,
And of him they all seem afraid.

Just so ; such is the end of those
Who meeteth in with adverse fate ;
Against us shut is every gate
When we the yellow " Geordies " lose.

But loss of money and of friends
Are nought compared to loss of mind ;
To Samuel fortune's been unkind,
But some day she may make amends

For what she's done unto him now,
And may reward him yet tenfold ;
This world the fallen feel it cold,
But to dame fortune all must bow.

IN MEMORIAM.—WILLIAM MARTIN.

A MELLOW harp has been unstrung,
And silent, too, the tuneful tongue
Of him who, like a seraph, sung,
And charmed us a' by Bowmont.

By that fair stream he often trod,
But o'er him now's the grassy sod,
And never more with gun or rod
Shall we him see by Bowmont.

The rabbits in yon stuntit wud
May cock fu' crouse their downy fud,
Nae mair we'll see him wi' his cud
In search of them by Bowmont.

The corbies noo may keep their nest,
And pyets too, and be at rest,
For ne'er again shall he molest
Those birds of prey by Bowmont.

Yon bick'ring grouse upon the hill
Will miss, I'm sure, the form of Bill,
For oft he watch'd wi' right good will
The poacher loons by Bowmont.

A better keeper than the bard
Was never laid beneath the sward ;
To find his equal would be hard, .
For a' folk on the Bowmont

Him lo'ed and likit as their ain,
And a' are sad that he is gane ;
With grief we've written on his stane,
" Here lies the bard of Bowmont."

Interred ere age had dimmed his e'e,
Just in his prime, I trow, was he ;
His like, I doubt, we'll never see
Upon the banks of Bowmont.

He had o' a' mankind the knack ;
Wi' tramps and gentlemen could crack ;
But death has laid him on his back,
And sound he sleeps by Bowmont.

Fu' well the beggars kent Dean Mill,
The curious home of poet Bill ;
Of cheese and bread aye got their fill
When he was there by Bowmont.

Of some he whiles would take the size,
And with them have a jolly rise ;
But those in want could not despise
The kindest soul on Bowmont.

He's been cut off in manhood's noon;
We're frail, and perish unco soon;
While at a friend's in Yetholm toon
Death snatch't the bard of Bowmont,

And wi' him sped unto that shore
Where many a one he's ta'en before;
And a' our hearts are sad and sore
Without poor Bill of Bowmont.

When August comes with all her train
Of dogs and gents. let loose amain,
Amongst them we shall look in vain
For him that's laid by Bowmont.

He was, 'tis said, a noble shot,
But o'er the moors nae mair he'll trot,
Nor lead their lordships to the spot
Where coveys sit by Bowmont.

Ah, no! ah, no! with such he's done,
And fire he'll ne'er another gun;
But Border land's proud of her son,
The keeper-bard of Bowmont.

While Bowmont doth his channels wet,
The bard that's gone we'll ne'er forget,
Till a' our suns, like his, be set,
To rise no more by Bowmont.

E M M A.

EMMA, wi' her thousand lovers,
  O' them a' she has the knack ;
When they ca' for ale or whisky,
  Wi' the change they get a smack.

Few are like her in the city,
  This the lads o' Teviot ken ;
Never was there such a lassie,
  She 's the airt o' a' the men.

Thousands bow the knee to Emma,
  Frae Satan she would steal the hairt ;
Be it so, I'll no' deny it,
  But, howe'er, I'll take her pairt.

After her in scores she leads them,
  Though they say 'tis for a drink ;
But, my certies, she knows better,
  For she has for a' a' wink.

Oh, the pawky, witchin' creature
  E'en has roused in me love's flame ;
And my ain sweet wifie won'ers
  What aye keeps me sae frae hame.

Fegs, my lads, I daurna tell her
  That fair Emma is the cause,
Lest she should come owre my hurdies
  For transgressin' sae the laws.

But for a' that, here's to Emma,
   For she knoweth how to sell
That stroug potion which the clergy
   Blame for makin' earth a hell.

GET GOLD, PURE GOLD.

GET gold, pure gold, all desperate dangers brave,
By fraud on land or plunder on the wave ;
Get gold, pure gold, no matter by what means,
Our faults and failings from the world it screens.

Get gold, pure gold, for of it all men dream
Within this age of dynamite and steam ;
Run through the world at twenty miles per minute,
And think of nought unless pure gold be in it.

Spin on till death, on precious gold rely,
Endow a church or college when you die ;
You but do that, what will the clergy say ?
A noble man or woman's passed away

Full of good deeds—perchance, who never gave
One penny to the poor this side the grave ;
Within the grassy churchyard next, I ween,
Uprise the stones to show the saints they've been.

Oh, world of wonders ! we, thy sons of clay,
Oft lose ourselves, and after pure gold stray ;
For gold, pure gold, the bashful clergy cry,
And woe to those who have and them deny.

Those that have nothing, and find life a fight,
Are told to give—the widow gave her mite;
For gold, pure gold, the hired assassins kill;
Yet without gold all commerce would stand still.

It wards off hunger, and it keeps out cold,
For all the wants of life depend on gold;
Get gold, pure gold, by just and honest means,
Our faults and failings from the world it screens.

DAVID TAIT, KIRK YETHOLM.

OH, take it not frae aff the wall,
　　That fiddle nor the bow;
Hush'd be it now, for cold the hand
　　Which made the music flow.
No more, my lads, shall we e'er dance
　　To the melodious strains
Which often made our hearts rejoice,
　　And blood warm in our veins.

Though others wake the giddy reel
　　Wi' notes that please the ear,
They cannot make us leap like him
　　Whom we all loved so dear.
Whene'er his fingers touched the strings,
　　Our bosoms filled with glee;
Oh! such a chield for mirth as him
　　Again we'll never see.

At weddings and at harvest homes
  He was a welcome guest;
Where'er he play'd his fiddle woke
  A joy in every breast;
He made old men forget their years,
  And matrons frail and grey
Would skip like lassies in their teens
  Whene'er they heard him play.

And we are more than sad this day
  To see his early tomb—
The " ace of hearts," the pride of men,
  Laid down in manhood's bloom.
His grave with flowers the fairest deck,
  For he was pure as them ;
Search as ye may, there's not a blot
  Upon his spotless name.

His fiddle there—oh ! let it hing
  A trophy for his sake ;
No other hand shall touch a string
  Of it here to awake
The memory of byegone days
  When he with us did fare ;
Hush'd be its chords, for ever hush'd,
  On it he'll play nae mair.

KEEPER JOCK.

Lang leggit Jess o' Cruikitshaws
    Regrets that she refused his offer ;
And smirkin' Jean o' Windywa's
    Oft tried to tempt him wi' her tocher ;
But, aha ! Jock, though fond o' fun,
    Kent love was aye the best o' riches,
And sae he sware, by moon and sun,
    That he would ha'e nae auld sour witches.

Sae aff he set to ane sixteen—
    Ye never saw a sweeter lassie :
Worth twenty o' baith Jess and Jean,
    And wi' him, fegs, she wasna saucy ;
She bade him welcome back again,
    Wi' love the lassie seemed quite smitten ;
But Jock has made her a' his ain,
    And by him noo she's crousely sittin'.

Upon his hearth wee bairnies rin,
    Whose voices fill the soul with pleasure,
And to our ears make pleasant din,
    For they are a' the poor man's treasure.
And Jock is happy as can be,
    With sons and daughters to him given ;
Nae trigger house could mortal see,
    For each man's house should be his heaven.

On Bowmont Water stands a house,
    A sonsie wifie in the door,
She has a baby in her arms,
    And others playin' on the floor,
And in the neuk sits the gudeman;
    Noo what think ye o' keeper Jock,
Blest wi' a wife and bairnies three,
    The sweetest flowers o' a' his flock?

A WANTER CROUSE.

WITHIN yon valley stands a house,
    And frae it comes the twisted smoke,
Within it lives a wanter crouse,
    And wha is he but keeper Jock?

He has a pony and a cart,
    Twa splendid kye upon the lea;
And a' he needs is but a heart
    To keep his ain in better glee.

Wi' him a wife micht happy be,
    Though he is but a sorry chiel;
He's nine gude pets as ye could see,
    And a' their lambs are dain' weel.

What though he's wearin' doon life's brae,
    His cheeks retain some tints o' simmer,
His head, losh me, is no' that grey,
    Sae he may get a couthie kimmer

To cheer him in his latter days.
  What's nicer than a peacefu' gloamin' ;
Youth's burning sun must cease to blaze,
  And he has had his fill o' roamin'.

The sturdy oak long, long may stand,
  And bid defiance to the blast,
But by and by time's cankering hand
  Will lay it in the dust at last.

M A N.

FRAIL mortal, tell me what art thou,
With heaven's seal upon thy brow,
    And feelings strong ?
The abject heir of care and pain,
Led here, now there, by reason's rein,
    And often wrong.

Between two paths of good and ill
Thou standest, and with wav'ring will
    Which often leads
Thee to the harvest field of grief,
Where thou must bind misfortune's sheaf
    Of useless weeds.

And thou hast been in life's fair hour
By tyrants trampled in the stour,
    And downward pressed ;

P

But rise thou up, be undismayed,
Yet man to mourn by man's oft made
    Must be confessed.

Frail mortal, thou of every ill
That can the cup of sorrow fill,
    And thou must drink
The bitter draught by spite instilled,
By puny man ordained and willed,
    But sad to think

That thou hast stood the stress and strain
So long upon life's stormy main,
    And thus, at last,
Wreck'd by a straw, and nothing more,
Upon the verge of a fair shore,
    Without a blast.

But there be that, and there is this,
For man, poor man, must bow and kiss
    The rod severe ;
So may thou live to see the day
When tyrants shall be laid in clay
    Without a tear.

With snares and lures on every side,
They try to trap, but never guide
    Thy steps aright ;
When up you've climbed the rough hill face
They'll bring you downward with disgrace,
    Such now thy plight.

Thy part is played, and thou shalt see
Those would-be gods as poor as thee,
    And more to mean,
Ere yet they die—Oh ! hear my prayer,
Thou who of all on earth tak'st care,
    Change Thou the scene.

THE ROSES.

THANKS for the roses you sent me,
    Around me still lingers the smell
Of the beautiful blooms, which remind me
    Of those in the dew-spangled dell.

Dear to my heart are the roses,
    And all flowers, whatever they be,
For I once had a sweet child that loved them—
    But now with the Saviour is he.

Oft do I gaze on the roses,
    Upon which the balmy dew lies ;
And oft do I water their petals
    With tears, which they never despise.

The roses you sent me I cherish,
    For in their sweet faces I see
The emblem of one who was taken
    Away from his mother and me.

Thou'rt a mother, I know, and hast tasted
   The sweets and the bitters of life;
For death, he is cruel, and cutteth
   The flowers that we love with his knife.

They say we should mourn, and not murmur—
   'Tis sinful, I know, to complain;
But all who have lost something precious
   Are anxious to have it again.

Just so, the same with the dear ones
   Who out of the circle we miss;
How fondly we cling to their last words,
   And think of the dear, parting kiss.

We're told that we'll meet them in heaven,
   And we hope that the promise is true;
But here back to us they'll return not,
   And dark is the glass we look through.

The roses, though watered and tended,
   Do wither and die in the vase;
And though they have lost all their beauty,
   Accept of this song in their praise.

POOR MAN.

Poor wretch, there's One who rules on high,
On Him for health and aid rely,
   And you'll get through;

For life's a battle at the best,
And man with man is ne'er at rest—
  Ah ! that is true.

The powerful just the weaker grind,
In every sphere you'll tyrants find,
  As I have found.
With tyrants mercy doth not bide,
Upon their fellow-men they ride
  On vantage ground.

For mercy I have sought in vain
From one for whom I've worn the chain
  Of menial slave ;
And thus I grieve to say in rhyme,
In bondage I have spent my prime,
  And like the lave

Of all his cast-off broken tools
I swell the list of countless fools
  Who have him serv'd
With heart and soul the same as me,
But this up-trip I do not see
  I it deserved.

But tyrant man shall have his way,
Despite of all I write or say,
  For he's the power ;
But fate is queer, and fate some day
This iron-hearted creature may
  Lay in the stour.

THE ROYAL STAPLERS.

THE Bowmont stream is wimplin' clear,
    For a' the clitter clatter
About the royal staplers here
    That dirty a' the water
Wi' clott'd clairts they gather in
    To renovate for weavin';
Though they in Bowmont get a synd,
    'Tis for an honest leevin'.

Ye rich, be mindfu' o' the puir,
    Wi' muckle they're tormentit;
And it'll swell the cat'logue mair
    If scourin' be preventit;
Sae let them get their taits o' woo
    Wash'd in the purlin' river,
Though they pollute it at the time
    It sune turns clear as ever.

Dae a' ye can to help the puir,
    Ye wealthy rural gentry;
O' Bowmont let them tak' a share,
    O' ither things ye've plenty:
Ye'll never miss the wee bit spot
    Where their machines are plantit,
And maybe yet ye'll wear a coat
    O' what they scour, sae grant it.

The ill they dae can be but sma',
    For trouts within the water

Appear to breed and thrive for a',
   And nane mair fresh and fatter·
Than those that jouk about the pools
   In simmer where they're washin';
Juist gang an' look, ye girnin' fools,
   And see the big anes splashin'.

Come wi' ye're rods, come wi' ye're creels,
   When ye ha'e time for sportin'';
The flees and lines frae aff ye're reels,
   They'll need but little courtin' :
The bait they catch wi' greedy gust,
   The clairts give them a cravin'
As great for food as they've gi'en me
   An appetite for ravin'.

Then let us hope to see again
   Our staplers on the channel,
And rowin' roon' wi' right good will
   The toilsome crusher's hannel ;
Sae let them wash and work awa'
   Within the ancient river
That murmurs through the flowery vale
   At clairts the same as ever.

THE BERWICKSHIRE SHEPHERD, WALTER CHISHOLM.

AH ! who can tell what dreams were his,
   In childhood, with his sheep ;

On high St. Abb's the infant bard,
In verse, first learned to creep.

The muses found him on that hill
Where purple heather waves
Above the bones of holy men
Within their moorland graves.

'Twas there Apollo warmed his breast,
And bade the music roll
From out the musical recess
Of his poetic soul.

Then in his teens, a happy lad,
The picture of good health,
With dog and plaid amongst the heath,
To him a monarch's wealth.

He painted nature in her robes
Of russet and of green,
And watch'd his flock wi' lightsome heart
From dewy morn till e'en.

Now hushed the harp on yonder hill
That charmed the evening hour,
When dew lay on the blushing rose
And on each tiny flower.

But fate ordained that he should go
Unto the bustling town,
Where fell disease upon him seized,
And laid the poet down.

BACHELOR WILLIE.

HE stamps air an' late through oor toon like a ghaist,
    An' some wadna care than say he is silly;
But, fegs, they are wrang wha ever think sae,
    For he's mair knave than fule, is Bachelor Willie.

An' though he is pass'd noo the summit o' life,
    At courtin' the lasses he's yet a great billy;
An' anxious he seems to get ane for a wife,
    But, somehoo, they a' laugh at Bachelor Willie.

He courtit Meg Pippins—I mind it fu' weel—
    An' she was as daft as a new yokit filly;
But she scorned the idea o' sic a queer chiel,
    An' upturn't her heels against Bachelor Willie.

Like a' slichtit lovers, he moaned an' he sighed,
    An' gaed aboot moppin', down-hairted, an' stilly,
While the young glaikit kimmers look't at him, an'
      cried,
    " Losh, what can be wrang wi' Bachelor Willie?"

He's plenty o' siller, an' women lo'e that,
    And though the young lasses may think his blude
      chilly,
He's married Nell Rough, wi' a beard like a cat,
    An' happy she seems wi' Bachelor Willie.

PRINCE NAPOLEON.

O'ER a hero's grave the muse doth weep,
With sword in hand he fell asleep,
   No more to wake.
He burned to achieve a warlike name,
And he gave his life for a little fame,
   A foolish stake.

Never envy those that aspire to a crown—
See the noble prince in his youth cut down,
   And laid in the dust,
With the spears of the foe transfixed in his breast,
For his dreams are o'er, and he's now at rest
   In the Lord, we trust.

In quest of fame he went to the war,
And France on him look'd as her rising star;
   But, alas! the scene
Has been changed, and changed to one of woe;
He is now in the mould, and lying low,
   With the sods on him green.

Of fame, proud fame, he shall dream no more,
And our hearts are rent to the very core,
   For we loved him dear;
A braver prince never lived before:
Oh, where were his men when the saddle tore,
   And the Zulus near?

Could they not have stayed in the hour of need ?
Forsaken by all, and his good grey steed—
   Oh, it left him too.
Could they not have stood, and around him died,
To save him ?—No, they never tried,
   But away they flew,

And left him alone with a savage horde,
Whom he faced, like Lochiel, with his own stout sword,
   . But they overcame
The hero-prince, and his patriot blood
Soon ebbed away in a crimson flood,
   To his comrades' shame.

THE SWALLOWS.

BACK again to Teviotside,
   And skimming o'er the valleys ;
For fairy spring ne'er fails to bring
   Us back the merry swallows
     To Teviotside.

And much we've missed them since they left
   Us in the autumn season,
But wi' them back the summer's come,
   And now the sun shines pleasin'
     On Teviotside.

The summer queen, with maiden air,
  Retreads the heights and hollows,
And in her train, on swiftest wing,
  With her have come the swallows
    To Teviotside.

Both far and near glad notes we hear,
  For a' the birds are singing ;
And here and there, through balmy air,
  Behold the swallows winging
    On Teviotside.

And them, I trow, we're proud to see
  Upon the riggin's resting,
Or darting out frae 'neath our eaves,
  Where they are busy nesting
    On Teviotside.

THE BOWMONT HILLS.

Of Bowmont stream I often dream,
  The Bowmont Hills I lo'e them yet;
To scenes long past I backward cast
  Mine eyes with fondness to them yet.

Oh, happy days ! for ever fled,
  Your shadows linger with me yet;
Like sweetest roses, plucked and dead,
  Their fragrance hovers round me yet.

Oh, Bowmontside ! how wildly grand,
　Thy cloud-capt mountains charm me yet ;
In fancy oft on them I stand,
　And feast me on thy valley yet.

Oh, Bowmontside ! thou fairy spot,
　To thee spell-bound I'm wholly yet,
And of thee now I'm rapt in thought
　By Teviot, where I musing sit.

Oh, land of glamour, glens, and streams,
　You fill my soul with rapture yet,
And bring'st me back a thousand dreams
　To glad me, where I musing sit.

Oh, Bowmontside ! what is't that binds
　My heart so firmly to thee yet ?
The cords of love round me you twine
　By Teviot, where I musing sit.

But let me wear those chains of love,
　I am not wearied of them yet ;
Oh, Bowmontside ! my bosom's pride,
　I lo'e thy men and maidens yet.

MY ALBUM.

My album, it is full of friends,
　I never had in it a foe ;
Their well-known photos ever tend
　To bind us to the long ago.

When all alone, 'tis sweet to sit
   And scan familiar faces o'er ;
Unspoken words surpass those writ,
   And touch our bosoms to the core.

Within my album hidden lies
   A language that I love to read ;
My friends, though mute, can make replies,
   And with me converse hold indeed.

On ilka page there is a friend
   Or dear companion far away ;
And photos to us shadows lend
   Of those who moulder in the clay.

Then sacred let us ever keep
   Those well known forms in far-off places ;
When all alone I sometimes weep,
   And bathe with tears familiar faces.

MY MOTHER.

THOUGH the heart be cold that loved me,
   And the tongue that pleased me still ;
My mother, can I e'er forget ?
   Ah, no ! I never will.

I'm lookin' back to other days,
   And I, in fancy, see
Her standin' by the little couch,
   Where oft she stood by me.

Far down the blighted vale of time
  I gaze with feelings warm;
Those days of childhood yet retain
  For me a hallowed charm.

Again I row upon the hearth,
  Where oft I've rowed before;
Now pu'in' roses off the bush
  That grew beside the door.

I feel the fragrance o' them yet,
  For nane e'er smelt sae sweet
As those that beautified the cot
  In which my heart first beat.

Here lookin' back to other days,
  Days to me ever dear,
It may be fancy, but I think
  Her mellow voice I hear.

I'm dreamin' noo, but let me dream,
  And feast on dreams like this;
About those days, long past and gone,
  There is a sacredness.

Whene'er I think upon those days
  Of innocence and mirth,
I feel as if transported back
  Unto the dear auld hearth

Where I the breath o' life first drew,
　And first the day did see:
Again I feel as when a child,
　Beneath my mither's e'e.

DECEMBER.

HAIL to the last month o' the year,
　December's aye a cauld ane;
And lordly John, that frosty seer,
　Among us struts a bauld ane.

In dreary short December days
　He's cankersome and grippy;
He nips our noses and our taes,
　And maketh roads richt slippy.

From place to place the carlin goes,
　And writes upon the water
A language that all nature knows,
　The birds it read and chatter.

Though gluttons dark December hail,
　And weary for the good things
Which they at Christmas-time assail,
　Regardless of the poor things

That chirp upon the leafless boughs,
　On which the sun's scarce blinkin',
And covered wi' December snow,
　While hoary John, unthinkin',

Puts his cauld hand upon their feet,
    Unhappit wi' a feather,
I wonder oft how they get meat
    In gloomy winter weather.

But there's a Hand we canna see,
    No matter how we gaze,
Deals out to them their daily food
    In dark December days.

THE PASSING YEAR.

THE passing year is dying fast,
Its winding sheet the stainless snow,
Spread out like linen white below,
In which it will be wrapped at last.

And soon the merry bells will ring,
To hail another bright and gay ;
The steeds of time still move away,
Though at the reins we tug and hing.

About the new we nothing ken,
The old one we ha'e draggled through—
Whiles unco sober, unco fou,
For there's no medium amongst men.

Yet with the years we onward pass,
Ne'er thinking that we're turning old,
Though in the Scriptures we are told
That all must perish like the grass.

Q

We forward look to coming years,
Though thin our locks may be and grey,
We hail with pride each New Year's Day,
For hope us on and upward bears.

And some who hailed the passing year
Are lying lowly in the clay ;
For them can come no New Year's Day,
Though some may have for them a tear.

THE LATE SERGEANT ROBERT AINSLIE.

THOU servant of great Nature's law—
Alas ! thou'st ta'en my friend awa' ;
Frae sorrows fount our tears ye draw,
    For a' folk likit Robert.

Abune him noo the sods are spread,
His years, threescore, for ever sped ;
On clay-cold pillow lies the head
    Of Robert ; yes, of Robert.

Such men as him earth ill can spare,
Without him Jethart looks quite bare ;
The echoes o' the court-room stair
    Lang for the feet o' Robert.

Up Castlegate the rogues he led—
Of him ill-doers had a dread ;
But it again he'll never tread,
    For in the dust lies Robert.

He was a man of worth indeed,
On pity's side did ever plead,
And young policemen tried to lead
   In the grand path of honour.

Weel may they sigh and a' lament
The blow that nane could e'er prevent;
But for his good 'twas maybe sent
   For Robert, sterlin' Robert.

Lord ! the bereft we leave to Thee,
To a' their wants Thy angels see,
The cup of comfort bid them pree,
   And cease to mourn for Robert.

Now safe with Christ for evermore,
His spirit treads the spirit shore,
And hither there the seraphs bore
   The immortal part of Robert.

Though in the grave we deem him fast,
Nought but his garments there was cast;
From death to life anew has passed
   The soul of honest Robert.

THE APPROACH OF WINTER.

In flocks the birds together keep,
And feast upon the ripened grain;
Of winter they might well complain,
And almost at his coming weep.

No more they pipe in early morn,
No more the craiks at evening call,
For yellow now the leaflets fall,
And summer's of her beauty shorn.

The swallows they have left the shed,
No longer on its rigging sit,
Nor round about the farm-house twit;
With summer they have from us fled.

The breath of autumn blights the rose,
The flowers are faded on the leas,
The birds are silent on the trees,
And all the leaves their greenness lose.

From out the north old winter comes
With all his storms in fierce array,
And fast the flowerets fade away,
On them no more the wild bee hums.

The wavy brackens, green and grand,
No more adorn the glen or hill,
For yellow autumn, wet and chill,
Has sered the sweets of all the land.

Within the hedgerows, dun and sere,
No more is heard the cheery notes
Of merry birds around our cots,
For icy winter's stepping near.

THE WIND KING.

WHEN the wind king awoke 'from his summer repose,
   He called to his captains, " For mischief prepare,
Yon crafts on the ocean dare not us oppose,"
   So around him he gathered his soldiers of air ;
         And thus he said,
           In his savage glee,
        " I'm lord of the land,
          And king of the sea."

Then to the woods with his army he went,
   Baying louder and fiercer than any bull ;
" Soldiers," he said, " let the trees be uprent,"
   For careless he seemed of decorum's rule.
         Yell after yell,
          The tall trees fell,
        And said, " My boys,
          You're fighting well."

Having slaughtered the woods, he hied to the main,
   And bathed his brow with the boiling spray,
For a terrible tempest wrought in his brain,
   And thus to his soldiers did boastfully say,
        " I've conquered the land,
         I'll conquer the sea,
        No pirate was ever
         So powerful as me."

And out on the beach brave women stood pale,
   While he scornfully laughed at them all undone ;

" O God, save the 'fishermen out in the gale,"
   Was the earnest prayer of every one.
         But he upset their boats
           With fiendish glee,
         And drowned the poor men
           In the raging sea.

Oh, thou cruel king, never come back again,
   And learn after this to be more wise ;
Yet from hotbeds of sorrow, anguish, and pain,
   Virtues the noblest often arise.

THE TENTIE HERD.

Oh, cruel death ! how could ye slay
The tentie herd, sae auld and grey,
And frae his flock tak' him away,
    By bonnie Tweed ;
Their bleatin' weel micht mak' ye wae,
    And rue the deed.

He was a herd, o' herds the best,
And unco kind to the distrest ;
Nae wonner that they cannot rest
    Since he is deid,
And wander, wearied and opprest,
    By bonnie Tweed.

For mony a day and year, I ween,
· He led them forth to pastures green,

And when the winds blew loud and keen
  About their heid,
He fand for them a cosy dean
  By bonnie Tweed.

Another herd the flock may tend,
And frae vile tods the lambs defend,
But, oh ! our hairts are like to rend,
  Since he is deid ;
Death's made a gap that nane can mend
  By bonnie Tweed.

Returning spring will soon display
Her vernal robes on mead and brae,
But, oh ! the herd that's in the clay,
  And cauld as leid,
Will ne'er return again to stray
  By bonnie Tweed.

The westlin' breeze may scented blaw,
When summer smiles and dewdrops fa',
But will that drive the gloom awa'
  That looms o'er Tweed ?
He was the king and ace o' a',
  The herd that's deid.

Oh, death ! how could ye strike the blow—
Ha'e ye nae pity ? See the woe
And the big tears that warmly flow
  For him that's deid ;
His like, I'm sure, ye ne'er laid low
  By bonnie Tweed.

·Exult not, grave, ye've but the case
That held the soul sae fu' o' grace,
A comet here amang his race
    He shone indeed ;
But now he's in a better place,
    The herd that's deid.

He needs no sculptur'd stone to tell
The hour and date on which he fell,
His worth to a' is known so well
    By bonnie Tweed ;
And when ye hear the Sabbath bell,
    Mind him that's deid.

KELSO: PRINTED BY RUTHERFURD & CRAIG.